"I'm sorry about the barn, okay?" the little girl said. "I didn't do anything bad. I didn't start the fire. I was just reading in there."

"I don't think the fire was your fault, Jessie," Mia told her. "It must have been an accident. Maybe electrical."

"Uh-uh. A man started it."

"What?"

The little girl trembled. "A really big man drove a truck into the barn. He got out and poured something stinky on the hay. Then he threw matches on it. He said, 'This ought to scare her.' Then he laughed and left. Do you think he meant me? To scare *me?*"

He didn't mean Jessie. He meant Mia. This was what the letter had warned her about. But who was this man?

"Jessie," Ryan called from the open doors. "Are you sure that's what you saw?"

"Uncle Ryan." Jessie's voice held relief. She charged into his arms.

Mia sat up, and her eyes connected with Ryan's troubled gaze. He pulled Jessie tighter and stared at Mia with the implicati̶o̶n̶ ̶o̶f̶ his face.

The fire was no accide̶

SUSAN SLEEMAN

grew up in a small Wisconsin town where she spent her summers reading Nancy Drew and developing a love of mystery and suspense books. Today she channels this enthusiasm into hosting the popular Internet Web site TheSuspenseZone.com and writing romantic suspense and mystery novels.

Much to her husband's chagrin, Susan loves to look at everyday situations and turn them into murder and mayhem scenarios for future novels. If you've met Susan, she has probably figured out a plausible way to kill you and get away with it.

Susan currently lives in Florida, but has had the pleasure of living in nine states. Her husband is a church music director and they have two beautiful daughters, a very special son-in-law and an adorable grandson. To learn more about Susan, please visit SusanSleeman.com.

HIGH-STAKES INHERITANCE

Susan Sleeman

Steeple
Hill®

Published by Steeple Hill Books™

STEEPLE HILL BOOKS

Steeple
Hill®

Recycling programs
for this product may
not exist in your area.

ISBN-13: 978-0-373-67432-9

HIGH-STAKES INHERITANCE

www.SteepleHill.com

Printed in U.S.A.

Trust in the Lord with all your heart and lean not on your own understanding.

—*Proverbs* 3:5

For my husband, Mark, who always believes in and encourages me to write, for Emma whose grasp of proper grammar has helped me more times than I can count, and for Erin, whose graphic design skills are priceless.

Acknowledgments

This book couldn't have been written without the help of others.

Thank you to fellow writers and all-around terrific friends, Sandra Robbins, Janelle Mowery, Elizabeth Ludwig and Marcia Gruver for sharing their writing expertise, thoughtful critiques and wise advice.

To Tina James, editor extraordinaire, thank you for selecting this manuscript and giving me a chance to tell this story. I am thrilled to be working with and learning from you.

For technical details, I give credit to the professionals who shared their time, patiently answering all my questions. Any errors in or liberties taken with the details are solely my doing.

Thank you to Taylor Woods, Program Supervisor/ Recruiter for SUWS of the Carolinas, for sharing his expertise in wilderness counseling programs.

To Lieutenant Shaun McNally, Richlandtown Fire Co. #1, who gave of his time to help me understand the complexity of fighting fires, I say a special thanks.

And most importantly, thank You, God, for my faith and for putting seemingly insurmountable challenges in my life to allow me to know without a doubt who is in charge of my life.

ONE

Pinetree will never be yours. Leave Logan Lake now or you will pay.

Mia Blackburn stared at the cutout magazine letters glued to stark white paper.

Was this some kind of a joke? Did someone really plan to hurt her for honoring her late uncle's wishes? To meet the terms of his will, she had agreed to live at Pinetree for the next year in order to inherit the resort. Yet nothing about the idyllic Oregon setting and worn cabins would garner this kind of threat.

With trembling hands, she flipped the envelope and searched for clues. The hate mail held a postmark from three days ago right here in the Logan Lake Post Office.

She rubbed a finger over the neat rows of shiny magazine letters. Anger seemed to leap from the page.

Her mouth went dry, and her throat tightened, nearly cutting off her air.

Only one person harbored such bitter feelings for

her. Her father. And knowing him, he'd lurk in the shadows to see her reaction to his threat.

The space seemed to darken with her thoughts.

Was he here, in the room watching her? Or would he be outside on Main Street, sitting in his Cadillac, drumming his fingers on the wheel as he did whenever he grew impatient?

The jarring clang of the front door bells ended her thoughts. She snapped her head up to see who entered.

Not her father, but just as bad. Maybe worse.

"Ryan." Her ex-boyfriend's name whispered out like a desperate plea for help as he strolled lazily into the space.

His warm expression and greetings spoke to his love of this small town and its people. He'd changed little since she'd last seen him at high school graduation. He was dressed in worn jeans, rugged boots and an army-green T-shirt that confirmed he hadn't quit working out. Curly russet hair had been cut short emphasizing his skin bronzed from the summer.

As if feeling her gaze, he turned in her direction. Recognition widened his piercing blue eyes. "Mia, is that you?" he called out with genuine fondness as if they'd parted best friends. He headed her way, giving her a quick once-over on the way. When his eyes returned to her face, appreciation radiated from his expression much like it had when they dated in high school.

"I almost didn't recognize you with the new look."

He reached out to lift a strand of her shoulder-length hair she'd straightened and dyed.

His touch shot a frisson of alarm through her far greater than the letter had. She searched for a reply, but gaped instead. He directed a counseling program that leased cabins at Pinetree in the off-season so she'd expected them to cross paths. However, she didn't count on freezing in place when she saw him again.

"I remember that look." His trademark crooked grin lit his face. "Got it every time I messed up."

This was too much. He was here…in front of her. The guy who'd hurt her like every man in her life except Uncle Wally. And she wasn't ready with the quick, witty comebacks she'd often visualized in her mind.

"You okay?" he asked.

"I'm fine." Fine? She wasn't fine. How was she going to get out of this situation?

She took a step back and focused on the waffle pattern in his T-shirt. This wasn't any better than peering into his eyes. The material stretched taut across his chest. A chest where she'd rested and received comfort after battles with her father.

"I'm sorry to hear about Wally," he said, filling the awkward space and bringing her gaze to his face. "I remember as a kid how I'd count down the days until he left Atlanta and came up here for the summer." A soft smile pulled at the corners of his mouth. "All the kids around here loved his camp.

Takes a special person to give so much time and money to help underprivileged kids like he did. I'm gonna miss him."

"Me, too," she managed.

Who was this woman taking over her body? Since their tumultuous breakup, she'd often visualized the strong woman she'd become, standing up to Ryan and releasing pent-up anger from the wounds he'd inflicted. Never did she see herself shying away like a terrified mouse.

So what? Even if she pulled herself together, this wasn't the time or place to get into their botched romance. Small towns had big ears and the last thing she needed was gossip about her served as the entrée on dinner tables tonight. She'd had enough of that in high school when she'd sparked the local gossip by rebelling against her father's rigid control, skipping school and partying all hours of the night.

Her best option was to cut this short. "If you'll excuse me, I really need to get out to Pinetree and unpack."

In search of car keys, she used her hip to shift her leather purse closer as she transferred the threatening letter to the other hand already bulging with envelopes. Shaking fingers fumbled and upset the pile, sending it crashing to the floor.

"Let me help." He dropped down and reached for the alarming letter.

No. He didn't need to see the warning.

She lunged toward the page, but his hand whispered

softly over hers and snatched up the paper. While he scanned the message, she slid the avalanche of envelopes into a stack.

"What's this?" His head lifted and deep crevices of concern burrowed into his face. "You can't seriously be thinking about going out there after receiving such a threat? We have to report this to the police, and you need to stay somewhere safe until they figure out who sent the letter."

How dare he express concern for her after the trauma he'd caused in her life!

She snatched the page from his hands. "Don't worry. Someone is just playing a practical joke."

Ignoring his confused expression, she bolted past him and into the crisp October morning. She didn't need Ryan worrying about or trying to take care of her. She'd been self-sufficient for years, and she didn't need a man—especially not *this* man—telling her what to do. She'd be fine.

"Mia, wait," he called after her. "You could be in danger."

Danger, ha! Talking to him was more dangerous than a vague warning. He'd hurt her once. She wasn't going to give him the chance to do it again.

Ryan watched as Mia charged away. After her reaction, his first instinct was to run in the other direction. Why bring up their past? Why not let things lie as they had for the last ten years?

Because her eyes seared him, that's why. Not with

the guilt he deserved but with a vulnerability that tugged at his need to help a woman in distress. Now she was charging away from him into danger. He couldn't let that happen.

He rushed after the click-clack of the skyscraper shoes she wore echoing down the street and into the sweet, tantalizing fragrance lingering behind.

Had his tomboy taken to wearing perfume?

She'd definitely given up the ratty jeans and slogan-boasting T-shirts she used to favor. Today, tailored blue jeans and a leather blazer emphasized her long, lanky body. Perfect on the current Mia who'd traded her mass of red curls for a sleek style that gleamed in the brilliant sunlight. Her hands shook as she inserted a key into the door of a sweet, red Mustang, but she still managed to climb into the car in record speed.

A car that would take her straight to Pinetree. She may not want anything to do with him, but he wouldn't let her race into danger just to spite him. He breathed deep to control rising emotions and stopped next to the car. She ignored him and lowered the convertible roof.

When the top cleared, he planted his hands on the door frame. "I get that you're still mad at me, Mia, but don't do something foolish just to get away from me."

She sat, rigid and unresponsive.

He leaned into her space. "Just give me a minute and then if you still want to go, I'll back off."

Her head slowly rose, and a shimmering strand of hair blew into her face. It would take some time for him to get used to her new look. Not that he didn't like it. Layered hair curved softly around her face, giving her a sophisticated appearance that was all too appealing.

He reached up to tuck the stray strand behind her ear, but she beat him to it and fixed tired eyes on his face.

"You have exactly one minute." She tapped her jeweled watch with a brightly painted nail.

The anguish in her gaze almost stopped his words. Almost. But he had to keep her safe. "It's crazy to go to Pinetree, sw—Mia." She didn't seem to notice his near use of sweetheart, or maybe she didn't remember or even care that he'd always called her that in high school. "You never know what the sender of this letter intends to do."

"I'm pretty sure it's from my father. You know how melodramatic he can get. If I leave town during the year, Pinetree defaults to David. So—"

"Wait. David gets Pinetree if you leave?" Ryan's tone pierced through the air. "It's got to be worth a bundle for the lakefront location. Seems like David is the logical person to want you to leave."

"I didn't say I was certain about my father. David is a possibility, but I doubt it." She sighed and closed her eyes for a moment as if she was humoring him. "David's firm handles Pinetree's finances so I've talked to him about the transition a couple of times in the last week. He said even though he was the older sibling, I deserved Pinetree because I was so much closer to Uncle Wally."

"How can you be sure he meant what he said? Maybe he was covering up his true feelings."

"His tone was sincere. Plus, he's never done anything in the past to hurt me, but Dad…" She released another sigh. "He's a different story. He always thought David was more deserving of everything, so why not this?" Her words were strong, but her voice trembled at the mention of her father and brother.

Ryan wanted to stroke her hair in comfort as he used to do after one of her father's many rampages, but he had no right. He'd seen to that.

He fisted his hands and searched for the words that would keep her away from Pinetree. But what could he say to make her see the danger she could be in?

Perhaps he had to paint a dire picture. "You may be right about the letter coming from your dad, but are you willing to risk your life on it?"

She recoiled as if he'd slapped her. "Your minute is up."

She fired up the car, and he reluctantly stepped back. He didn't know why she'd reacted so strongly but he did know he'd failed her again. Was he destined to fail her at every turn? He shook his head and watched her back out of the space.

At least this time he had God to turn to. He never disappointed anyone.

Ryan focused on the impressive stand of Douglas firs in the distance.

Lord, please keep Mia safe. And if it is your will, let her see my sincere desire to apologize for how I hurt her and help her to forgive me for what I did.

At the screech of tires, his head snapped back, and he watched the car shoot down the street. Despite the ache her resentment left behind, the familiar sight brought a brief smile. Mia might dress all prissy and girly now, but she remembered how to drive like a guy.

Oh, yeah, she'd always been a little spitfire. Rebelling against her father. Getting into trouble left and right. Calming down some the year they were together. Taking up again when they split up to show everyone she didn't need him.

And she didn't need him. Not now, anyway. He'd hurt her by how he'd handled the breakup, that was for sure, and he wanted to fix it. Now more than ever. Seeing her dredged up the horrible day they'd parted, and he needed to explain why he had to end things as he had. To seek her forgiveness so he could put this to rest.

Instincts and the desire to do the right thing with Mia told him to jump in his truck and follow her to Pinetree, but the threatening message urged him to go see Russ, his brother and chief of police. He could talk with Mia later, but not if the person behind the letter made good on his threat and harmed her in the process.

* * *

Leave Logan Lake now or you will pay...

The barn, dry from a typical rainless summer, flared in oranges and reds as if a meteor had streaked from the sky and plunged into the building.

Had he done this? Had he really made good on the threat?

Dense smoke clung to Pinetree's sign and surrounding treetops like cotton candy on a stick. The air was laden with fumes, not the sort of pleasant scents drifting from a campfire, but serious gusts of blackness settling into the open car and irritating her breathing.

Heart beating erratically, Mia remembered the advice of the 911 operator she'd just called. She should move to a safe location and wait for the fire department to arrive. But what if Uncle Wally still kept horses in the barn? If they were trapped she couldn't sit here and listen to them cry out. She had to try to rescue them. She kicked off her heels and scrambled from the car.

Listening for cries of distress, she ran the length of the barn and circled the backside. Embers shot into the air. Explosions—bullet-like pings—struck the walls. The heat and caustic air seared her lungs. Howling screams from the consuming fire eased and the heat receded a bit, allowing her to inch closer to the acrid smoke seeping through cracks in the walls.

What was that? A whimper. Quiet. Muffled. Her imagination?

She stopped and leaned closer to a window, panting from exertion and the thickened air.

There it was again. A terrified mewl. A kitten or maybe a small child.

With a large rock, she shattered the window. Blistering heat whooshed out sending her lurching back. She ripped off her jacket and held it in front of her face.

"Is someone there?" she called, and swiped thick sweat from her forehead.

"Help!" The voice was tiny and high, fragile like a porcelain doll.

Who in the world was in there?

Jacket over her fingers, Mia cleared the largest shards of glass and plunged her head through the opening. Her eyes instantly watered, her nose stung.

"Where are you?" she barked through drying lips, and squinted against the bitter smoke.

A petite tear-stained face peeked from a cave of hay bales. Mia guessed the innocent child to be under ten and terrified.

"Don't be afraid." Ignoring the abrasive air and drawing in labored breaths, Mia lowered her jacket and offered a comforting smile as she scanned the space.

This end of the barn was quickly filling with smoke. She glanced to the left where a pickup truck had succumbed to searing flames. If anyone was in the truck there was no hope, but the child was another story. She'd coax the girl to the window, and avoid a terrible tragedy.

"Come here, sweetie." Mia curled her index finger. "Everything's gonna be all right."

The girl blinked in rapid succession then wailed like the fire siren Mia wished she'd hear screaming up the drive. Sobbing increasing, the child darted back into her hiding spot.

"No! No! Don't do that," Mia cried as fear coursed through her body. She would have to go in and carry the girl to the window.

She planted her hands on the frame and slithered over the windowsill, shards of glass ripping into her stomach. Pain stabbed her side but she inched forward and pushed aside hay bales. The child burrowed deeper into the haven like a baby animal threatened by a predator.

Mia leaned in and forced a calm tone to her voice. "Hi, my name's Mia. What's yours?"

"J-J-Jessie Morgan." Her voice was raspy.

Mia startled at the mention of the Morgan name. Was this child related to Ryan?

Jessie coughed hard enough to launch an entire country from her throat.

Not a time to think about Ryan, Mia needed to get Jessie out of there fast. "If you'll let me, I'll carry you to the window."

Jessie nodded and flung her arms around Mia's

neck. The pungent smell of smoke clung to her soft blond hair, and her little body trembled. Mia draped her jacket over their heads and turned to the window. The roof over the truck collapsed sending a blazing support beam into the path between the fort and their escape. Sparks shot toward the rafters. The flaming wood ignited dry hay.

Jessie's mouth opened in a scream, but only a deep wracking cough surged out. She clutched Mia tighter. Mia frantically looked for a way out. The window was no longer an option, and the back door sported huge chains. Panic surged. Her hands shook.

Where could they go?

She scanned the only wall not engulfed in flames. There! In the door. Uncle Wally installed a pet door when he got Rufus. The opening wasn't big enough for her, but Jessie could easily fit through.

Mia jumped from the bales and rushed to the back door. Lungs seared from smoke and exertion reduced her oxygen levels, and her eyesight wavered. She dug deep for strength and ripped off the pet door's pliable flap. "Okay, Jessie. Climb through."

Jessie planted her feet and crossed her arms.

"Sweetie, please." An instinctive coo rose to Mia's lips. "I'd come with you but I can't fit through the opening. Once you get outside, you can go to the lodge to wait for help. I called the fire department and they'll be here soon." Though frightened that the all-volunteer crew might not arrive in a timely manner, Mia smiled to ease Jessie's concern.

"My Uncle Ryan's a fireman." A tentative smile crept across her lips, and her stance relaxed.

Mia ignored the knifelike pain Ryan's name rekindled in her stomach and forced calm into her voice. "Good. He's probably on his way here to help us."

She gave Jessie a quick hug then helped her climb to safety.

Turning sideways, Mia wedged her body into the opening. Through cracked lips, she gulped outside air. Although tainted, it was less dense—easier to breathe.

Jessie stood beside the door as if concrete encased her feet.

"Jessie," Mia tugged on the girl's ankle, "go to the porch and wait until your uncle comes for you."

She nodded, but didn't move.

"Go, now!" Mia shouted, though it pained her to yell at this physically and emotionally exhausted child.

Jessie snapped from her daze. "I'll bring Uncle Ryan to help when he gets here."

Mia nodded her approval and watched until the plodding little feet moved out of sight. The last thing Mia needed was for Ryan to come to her rescue and be indebted to him. She'd have to try harder to get herself out of this mess.

She pulled her head back inside and looked around. Thirty feet to the wall of flames. Thirty feet of hay and dry timber waiting for fire to consume and destroy.

She searched again for another way out. Sizzling flames obliterated the path to the window and the front door. A miracle or the doggie door were her only ways out.

Please, I can't handle this right now. Coming back here is all I can manage. This is too much.

Why was she calling out to God? He'd never helped before. No—she was on her own again the way God seemed to like it. Well, she wouldn't just lie down and die.

Drawing her legs up, she crammed her upper body back through the opening. The frame tore at the gash on her side. She bit her lip to control the pain as she squirmed and twisted.

Right, left, up, down, she pushed. Nothing.

"Face it, Mia, you're stuck." She relaxed to conserve her energy for another try and the irony of her situation struck her as funny. She laughed in tiny giggles that foretold a meltdown.

She'd summoned up all her courage to return to Logan Lake and face the people who'd hurt her the most, only to die in a fire.

TWO

Ryan's two-way pager continued to emit details of the fire from the holder on his hip. No need to listen. He had all the information he needed. He tuned out the chatter and focused on Jessie's terrified eyes begging him to stay.

"I have to help Mia," he said, giving the sweet eight-year-old a comforting smile. He pulled her close for a brief hug. "Dupree will stay with you until I get back."

He hated to leave this little squirt with the EMT, but he had no choice. The rest of his crew hadn't arrived, and Mia might die before they did. He gave Jessie one last lingering look then rushed toward the barn.

Surging flames consumed half the building cracking and spitting out glowing embers. Life-sucking flames.

Man. This was bad. Really bad. Hopefully he wasn't too late. Not like that horrible day three years ago.

No. Don't think about that now. Today you're on time. You will save her life.

Clumsy in his boots and turnouts, he charged at the radiating heat. He lowered his face shield and dodged raining debris like an Olympic hurdler.

Thankfully, Russ hadn't been in the office, or Ryan would've been sitting there when his pager went off. The drive would have taken fifteen minutes. No one would be here to rescue Mia from the flames steadily licking forward in search of fresh fuel. He'd have another tragedy on his hands. He had to hurry.

He careened around the corner.

Whoa! There she was. Mia. His Mia. Crumpled and protruding from a pet door. But she was breathing. Alive. He should be able to pry her free before the flames reached her, but smoke inhalation could still claim her life.

His steps faltered. Uncertainty settled over him like the thick smoke billowing from the barn. This was too close for comfort.

God, don't let this end as it did with Cara.

Ryan felt God's strength surrounding him and urging him forward.

"Are you all right?" he called to Mia.

She craned her neck up at him, and her eyes fluttered open. Large green emeralds glistened likely from smoke-induced tears. "Did you find Jessie? Is she okay?"

Yeah, this was his Mia all right. Always concerned for others in distress. "Jess is fine. She's with the EMTs."

"Good, I wanted to—" A harsh cough tore away her words. The spasm intensified, racking her body.

This wasn't good. With the way he ended things between them, a stubborn Mia would rather die in the fire than let him come to her rescue. She couldn't know his identity.

He pulled his gaze away and studied the door. He'd use his pry bar to splinter the wood above her head and drag her to safety. At least he hoped his pry bar was tool enough to do the job. There was no one else to help and the blaze flared around them.

"Hold on, sweetheart." Years of unspoken affection flowed unbidden through his tone. "I'm gonna get you out of there."

Sweetheart? Was this guy kidding? She was trapped in a fire, struggling to breathe, and he patronized her with a chauvinist comment? She hated when men talked down to women.

A spark of recognition shot through her. Wait! Maybe it was Ryan. He used to call her sweetheart.

Nah. After the way they broke up, he wouldn't dare use that endearment in her presence. Besides, Ryan would have identified himself.

"Keep your head down." His bold tone spoke to his confidence and helped ease her concerns.

She fixed her eyes on his heavy black boots as rippling shocks traveled down the wood. Waves of pain reverberated into her injured side. She bit her lip. Held it fast between clamped teeth. One last tremor. Her body lurched forward, plunged toward the dirt. The metal tool thunked on the ground, and her freefall stopped.

"Got you," he said, clutching her under the arms. "Think you can stand?"

"My legs are numb."

"Then I'll have to carry you." He didn't wait for her agreement but in one swift motion, pulled her free then slipped his hands under her legs.

Sirens screamed in the background as he gently settled her against his broad chest. His jacket reeked of burnt wood and scratched roughly against her skin.

Didn't matter. Not a bit. She was out of that door. Snuggled warm against his chest. He drew her even closer. Umm, nice. She was safe. It had been so long since she'd felt safe like this. Not since she and Ryan were together.

What was with her? Back in town for a few hours and all she could think about was the man who'd sent her running away in pain. Not a good idea to go there. She concentrated on breathing the improving air into aching lungs.

The wall he'd freed her from groaned and shuttered as if heaving a last breath. He picked up speed and crossed the grass with sure footing until they arrived at a dented white pickup.

Squatting, he settled her against a rusted wheel

well. "There you go. Not too comfortable, but it will have to do for now."

"Thank you. If you hadn't come along, I—" Her voice broke, and she couldn't speak. She changed her focus to the screaming red truck bouncing down the driveway, followed by several personal vehicles.

He squeezed her shoulder, and she turned back.

"You doin' all right?" He flipped up his visor and fixed penetrating blue eyes on her.

It *was* Ryan. Her Ryan.

No, he hadn't been her Ryan for years. This was the man who hurt her and now she owed him her life.

"I know you're upset with me, Mia, but we have to put aside our differences and talk about the letter. The fire changes everything. You have to admit the letter wasn't just a practical joke."

"You're jumping to conclusions." Conclusions she'd reached, but wouldn't speak aloud. "The fire could've started on its own."

"Possibly." He crooked his thumb at the barn. "Won't take long until we know for sure. Until then, I want you to stay away from Pinetree."

She sighed and leaned her head against the truck. She was so tired. Tired of carrying around the baggage of their breakup and now she'd do just about anything to make the heartache go away.

Even if it meant letting him help her through this… But she couldn't trust him. Any man for that matter. They only disappointed her with their need to control and then bailed on her when she didn't let them take charge.

She had to keep up the wall, or he'd hurt her again. "I really don't want to talk about this with you."

Laying a gentle hand on her cheek, he turned her to face him. "You're letting your anger at me cloud the issue, and you're acting reckless."

She let his hand linger like a caress. The tender warmth felt right. Like old times, before the breakup. When she thought they'd be together forever. When she believed in the pure love of a man. When she could afford to take chances.

She shook his hand off. "My safety is none of your concern."

"Given the way I treated you I can understand how you could think that, but I don't want to see you get hurt." He lifted his helmet and ran a hand over sweaty hair. "We should call Russ and tell him about the threat."

"Russ?"

"He's the police chief now. He can help."

"I don't want anyone to know about this. I'll handle it my way."

"But this is too—"

"I said no! I don't want everyone in town gossiping about me on my first day back. If you care about me like you said, you'll keep this to yourself." She locked her eyes on his. "Promise me you won't tell him. Or anyone. You owe me that much."

"Fine." He let out a frustrated breath. "I'll go along

with you, but you should reconsider and tell him yourself."

"She okay, Morgan?" A firefighter with Chief lettered on his helmet hustled toward them, breaking the mood.

Ryan stood but kept his gaze glued on hers. "I sure hope so." His double meaning didn't escape her, but she forced back her feelings.

"You the only one in the barn?" The chief directed his question at her.

"I think so," Mia said, blocking out Ryan and paying full attention to the chief. "There's a truck in there, but it was completely engulfed in flames. I don't know if anyone was in it, but at least Jessie got out safely."

The chief faced Ryan. "Morgan, you go help Becker investigate that truck. Dupree can take care of Mia for now."

"I'm on it." Ryan let his eyes linger long enough to tug Mia's emotions back to life, then he took off.

As much as she tried, Mia couldn't keep her focus from Ryan battling his way into the south end of the building. Fear equal to finding Jessie trapped in the blaze crept over her. He was risking his life to check the truck for survivors. Something brave firefighters did every day. But her heart didn't clutch under her ribs for those firefighters.

What was up with that anyway? Did she have residual feelings for him or had his kind, compassionate eyes caught her off-guard like they always had in the past?

One of the EMTs plopped down next to her, ending Ryan's captivating pull.

Good. Now she could get her mind off him and on to figuring out how to follow up on the fire. She'd do what she always did, organize and control her steps so she didn't let feelings get in her way. With Ryan threatening her emotional stability, she was going to need an extra-detailed plan so he didn't derail her from her quest.

Planting his feet wide apart, Ryan gripped the pulsing hose and trained the spray in front of Becker as he neared the truck. Becker picked his way through the smoldering ruins and flare-ups before giving a thumbs-up indicating the truck was clear. No lives were lost in the fire today.

A wave of relief washed over Ryan as he turned the hose over to the other fireman and headed for the chief to tell him the news. Today had been a good day.

Being a firefighter in a small town meant if someone perished in a fire, you likely went to school with them, or to church—or served on a committee together. Worst case, you were related or in love with the person, maybe planning to marry.

Like Cara. Except she didn't die in a fire. A madman ended her life. Much like the lunatic threatening Mia might do.

Ryan halted his steps and fixed his gaze on her. Even beaten down by her ordeal she had the same vibrancy in her personality as he remembered from high school. Sure she'd been unstable in so many ways back then, but her longing to be loved by her uncaring father fueled that behavior. Ryan had hoped his unconditional acceptance of her might have been enough. But it wasn't. Couldn't fill the ache left by the loss of her mother and an overbearing father.

Eyes fixed on her, Ryan resumed walking. He'd been wrong. So wrong to end things the way he did. Now he didn't know how to get her to hear him out. He should just walk away with his guilt firmly planted in his gut. She didn't deserve to relive the day just to relieve his suffering, but he had no choice.

If he had to make her suffer a little more so she'd listen to his warnings before the lunatic behind the threatening letter and the fire struck again, then that's what he would do.

THREE

A blustery gust of wind kicked up from the north and slid crisply over Mia. Not that she minded the cooling air after the heat of the fire. Didn't seem to bother EMT Sally Dupree either as she strapped a blood pressure cuff on Mia's arm. She relaxed and let her gaze drift to Jessie.

Sally's partner ministered to the pipsqueak of a girl who didn't stop asking questions about the procedures. Her tone was lighthearted, and she cracked up when the EMT tickled her, but a haunted glaze dulled the sheen of her eyes.

Mia had no desire to laugh after what she'd just survived, not even if it was forced. As a counselor, she knew kids had the ability to recover faster from trauma than adults. Children could also appear to be fine but suffer tremendous emotional scars. She would make a point of telling Jessie's parents about signs that indicated Jessie had a residual problem.

"Do you know if anyone notified Jessie's parents?" Mia asked.

"Jessie's mother died a year ago, but I'm sure

someone called Reid, and he'll be here soon." Sally frowned and planted her stethoscope on Mia's chest. "Deep breaths."

Feeling a kindred connection from the death of a mother, Mia studied Jessie more intently. Her shoulders drooped in defeat and her gaze skittered about as if fearing an attack from an unknown force.

Today's trauma coupled with the recent loss of her mother could plummet Jessie into a depression. Hopefully Reid parented Jessie better than Mia's dad had her when her mother died, or the child could be destined for a rocky adolescence.

Sally pulled her stethoscope free and tsked. "We need to get you to the hospital."

No. Not the hospital!

Her father would be there.

Mia sat up. "I'd rather not go, unless it's absolutely necessary."

"Trust me. It's necessary." Sally's somber tone left no room for argument. She summoned her partner on a radio then strapped a mask over Mia's mouth.

She inhaled the cool oxygen and tried to relax even as pain ripped into her side from the transfer to the gurney and trip into the ambulance. She offered a smile at Jessie sitting on a bench seat below a wall of equipment. Jessie's eyes mirrored Mia's emotions, and she returned the smile with an uneasy stare.

After the EMTs secured the gurney and stepped to the end of the ambulance, Jessie jumped down and knelt near Mia's head.

"Don't tell anyone I was in the barn," Jessie whispered in Mia's ear.

Mia lifted her mask. "You weren't supposed to be in there?"

"No." Jessie clasped her hands together and stared at them. "Since my mom died, everybody says I shouldn't be alone so much. But I like to be alone so I can read."

Mia was thirteen when her own mother died in a car accident, but that first year after the accident, the constant ache never left her heart. Not to mention living the next five years with a father who blamed her for causing the crash that took her mother's life.

"Mia, will you promise not to tell?" Jessie tugged on Mia's arm, bringing her back.

Mia wanted to give this poor motherless child anything she asked for, but she couldn't. "I don't need to tell anyone, Jessie. They already know you were in the barn, or you wouldn't be in here with me."

"I could say I came in to save you."

Mia's counseling instincts shot into action. Jessie was hiding something. Her pained expression conveyed there was much more at stake than her father learning she'd been somewhere she wasn't supposed to be.

"What's this really about?" Mia clasped Jessie's miniature hands.

She shook them free, and her eyes took on a

defiant tightness. "I'm sorry about the barn, okay? I didn't do anything bad. I didn't start the fire. I was just reading. Wally used to let me read in the barn whenever I wanted to."

"I don't think the fire was your fault. It must have been an accident. Maybe electrical."

"Uh-uh. A man started it."

"What?"

Jessie trembled. "A really big man drove a truck into the barn. He got out and poured something stinky on the hay. Then he threw matches on it. He said, 'This ought to scare her.' Then he laughed and left." Her eyes scrunched as she rubbed her hands together. "Do you think he meant me? To scare *me?*"

He didn't mean Jessie. He meant Mia. This was what the letter warned her about. But who was this man? Had her father hired him? Or perhaps the letter wasn't from her father after all?

"Jessie," Ryan called from the open doors. "Are you sure that's what you saw?"

"Uncle Ryan." Jessie's voice held relief. She hopped up and moved slowly toward the back. "Honest, that's what I saw. You're not mad that I was in the barn?" She peered at Ryan until his face broke in a warm smile, and he beckoned her closer with his finger. She charged into his arms.

Mia sat up, and her eyes connected with Ryan's troubled expression. He pulled Jessie tighter and stared at Mia with the implication of Jessie's words stamped on his face.

The fire was no accident.

Still dressed in his turnouts, Ryan sat on the bench running the length of the ambulance. Even with his boots firmly planted on the floor, he bounced on the seat from the rhythmic beat of the tires spinning over rough pavement. The space was tight, but Jessie had begged him to ride with her to the hospital. Dupree had succumbed to Jessie's pleas and she'd moved things around to accommodate the four of them.

Jessie rested on his lap, reclining back with her head crooked in his arm. He stroked her sooty hair. He'd do anything to distract her from the residual terror in her eyes. Her emotional state was tenuous at best.

Then there was Mia.

He raised his head and subtly checked her out. She'd closed her expressive eyes and breathed through the oxygen mask. He let his eyes linger on the uncharacteristically quiet woman. What a brave front she displayed for Jessie. She kept it together, but the creases in her forehead exposed her internal pain.

The EMT said Mia should physically recover after a short course of oxygen. She was lucky. She'd lived when others died. He'd dragged her from a near death. From searing flames.

He let out a shaky breath and raised his head.

Thank you, Lord for sparing Mia's life.

But was she out of danger?

Had the fire merely been the first of a chain of events that would escalate until she left Pinetree or was killed for staying? How could she refuse to seek Russ's help, and forbid Ryan from doing so?

Especially after Jessie confirmed the fire was an act of arson.

He had to find a way to get Mia to talk to Russ before the danger he was certain lurked around the corner caught up with her.

Mia felt the warmth of Ryan's gaze, and she wanted to open her eyes to see what his face might reveal about his thoughts. But she wouldn't look, couldn't look, in case she saw the same horrified expression that had consumed his face when Jessie confirmed the fire was set on purpose. If she did, her fear would ratchet up to an unbearable level.

A stranger wanted her gone.

But who and why? The only logical explanation was that her father didn't want to get his hands dirty so he hired the baldheaded guy to torch the barn.

He was going to extreme lengths to get her to leave Pinetree, but as much as she was afraid of what might happen if she stayed, she wasn't going home. She owed it to Uncle Wally—the only man who truly loved her—to fulfill his last wishes.

Yes, she would stay in Logan Lake even though staying meant living near the man whose eyes were burrowing into her right now. Not just any man. Ryan. Her one-time protector. The man who made her feel safe again as he carried her securely from the barn. His strength almost let her believe he could make this horrible day go away. That she would be okay.

His phone pealed, and she flashed open her eyes, catching his tender gaze fixed on her. She felt her cheeks flush and a warmth spread through her body.

"It's the ringtone for work, and I have to take the call." He smiled wide revealing teeth that hadn't needed any dental assistance to be perfect. He'd often used this cute little grin when she'd glanced up and caught appreciative looks from him in the past.

As he pulled the phone free, she closed her eyes again. He may have saved her life, but he was still a man and like all men, he'd hurt her once. He'd do the same thing again if she gave him a chance.

As Ryan had expected, caller ID identified Ian Davis, his assistant at Wilderness Ways. Ryan was the director of the outdoor counseling program for wayward teens, and no matter the turmoil in his life, responsibility for the students dictated he answer.

He clicked Talk. "Ian, what's up?"

"We have a problem." Ian's serious tone set Ryan on edge. "Paul just called. His mother slipped into a coma this morning, and he won't make the first week of the program, if he comes at all."

Man. This was all Ryan needed. With the drop in funding, he'd already had to cut one staff member, and up the ratio of students to counselor. One less counselor and the kids had a better chance of ending up back in juvie than working through their issues, ultimately dooming this pilot program for juvenile offenders.

Not wanting to increase the anxiety level cutting through the ambulance, Ryan fought to keep the turmoil out of his voice. "How's Paul holding up?"

"Says he's okay, but you know, man. He's hurting."

"Make sure he knows we'll pray for him."

"Already done." A breathy intake of air and long exhale followed the clipped words. "We have to figure out what to do. There's no way we can function being down another counselor."

"You have any ideas?" Ryan asked.

"One, but I'm not sure you're gonna like it."

Ryan tucked the phone under his chin and used his free hand to massage a tight muscle in his neck. "Tell me about it. Doesn't matter if I don't like it."

"Okay, but hear me out before you shoot me down." Ian paused as if he thought Ryan might object.

Ryan would consider anything if it helped the kids. "Go on."

"The other day when we were talking about that Mia chick taking over Pinetree, you said she was a counselor. I know there's some sort of history between the two of you, but you could ask her to fill in until Paul gets here."

Ryan let his free hand fall to the bench with a thud. His stomach sank along with it. He looked at Mia. He was all for making amends for the way he'd botched their breakup, but how could he handle her daily presence at work? Living with the constant reminder of his mistake.

Easy answer—he couldn't. "I don't think—"

"I knew you wouldn't like it," Ian said. "But you have to admit, it's a good idea. She has no wilderness counseling experience, but she does work with teens. You can at least think about it, right?"

"What about training? Our program is unique and she hasn't participated in anything like it."

"We've got enough time before the students get here to bring her up to speed. Even without experience she'd be better for the students than no one."

Ian was right; Ryan had to think about what was best for the kids. "I'll give it some thought."

"Don't take too long. The kids get here in two days."

Ryan said goodbye and clicked off. He didn't need a reminder of the looming deadline and the need to decide quickly.

He stowed his cell, and let his focus return to Mia. Her appearance had changed since high school, but man, she was still a knockout. And that's what the many lacerations and bruises dotting her body did to him. Sent knockout punches to his gut. She could have died in the barn if he hadn't arrived when he did. He would never have had a chance to talk to her. Never had a chance to right the wrong he'd inflicted.

He had to make things right with Mia—and the best way to get her to listen to him was to spend time with her. As a bonus, it gave him an excuse to keep her in his sight. To keep her from stepping recklessly into whatever danger loomed ahead.

FOUR

In the miniscule hospital bathroom, Mia moved her portable IV cart to the side and stepped up to the sink. Without a shower, she'd make little progress in fixing her appearance but she couldn't spend the night without doing something. She'd hoped for a quick in and out in the ER, but due to continued low oxygen levels, the doctor opted to keep her overnight as a precaution.

With stiff fingers, she scrubbed her face. The pore-clogging soot not removed by the nurse's antiseptic clung to her skin. No matter the amount of scrubbing, the steaming hot cloth wouldn't wipe away emotional trauma. As if she knew what to wipe away first. She had so many layers.

Did she start with the memory of finding Jessie trapped in the barn and nearly losing her own life? Or the sappy way she'd reacted to Ryan? How about the fact that the fire wasn't an accident? Or her father's possible role in this disaster?

She leaned closer to the mirror and gently dabbed around sutured lacerations on her cheek.

Had her father really done this to her? As a teen he'd ignored her, blamed her for suggesting a ride in the country, and then distracting him while driving so he let the car slip off the shoulder and crash into a tree killing her mother on impact.

But was he so cruel that he could hire a man to commit arson in an attempt to scare her away? And if he did, how was she going to prove it? No one in town would entertain the thought that the good doctor Thomas Blackburn moonlighted as a criminal.

"Mia, you in there?" a male voice, deep and vaguely familiar, called from her room. "I need to talk to you."

She hated anyone to see her in this condition, but his urgent tone moved her to respond. "Be out in a minute."

She draped the cloth on the sink and finger combed her hair. Yuck. It would take several shampoos to eliminate the stench and caked-in ashes. She replaced the oxygen cannula in her nose and on the way out, freed the plastic tube stuck under the IV cart.

Standing by the door, her visitor wore a khaki police uniform and kneaded his shoulder with narrow fingers. He studied her, taking in every detail as she eased into the room. His presence was intimidating, drawing the air from the room.

Eyes fixed on her, he offered a stiff smile. "Don't

know how we'll ever repay you for saving our little Jessie."

His Jessie?

Mia checked his eyes. Oh, yeah. He was a Morgan. Even without the uniform, she'd know this was Ryan's brother Russ.

The tallest of the Morgan brothers, he was more powerfully built than she'd remembered. Coppery hair had grayed at the temples, but retained a bit of the Morgan curl at the nape. His eyes were clouded, maybe in reaction to nearly losing his niece.

Trauma Mia knew all too well. Fire sizzling all around and no rescue in sight. She suppressed a shiver. "I don't need any thanks for helping Jessie. I'm just glad I came along when I did."

"How about we sit?" He gestured at the pair of gray vinyl chairs by the window and issued a full smile, broadening an already wide jaw. The lines circling his eyes and folds along his nose—likely from the stress of a career in law enforcement—fell away, and the teenager she used to know bloomed in front of her.

Not that seeing the teen who tormented her was a good thing. Still, she needed to know what he wanted with her.

Lifting her oxygen lifeline over the bed, she navigated the tank toward the chair and sat.

"It's been a long time since we've seen you around here." He perched a booted foot on the wooden edge of the other chair. "With the way you shot out of here after high school, I'm surprised you came back. Guess it's hard to turn down the money you'll get when you sell Pinetree."

Did he think she'd react to his cutting tone? Or his assumption that she'd sell Pinetree at the end of the year to capitalize on the valuable lakefront property? Snap judgments were common around here. Just another reason she'd stayed away. Still, she wouldn't correct them. She knew in her heart she'd returned to Pinetree out of respect for her uncle's last wishes. That was all that mattered.

"If you're trying to bait me like you used to, Russ, I'm not biting."

"I'm here to take your statement about the fire. Nothing more."

"Sounded more like you were interested in passing judgment on me. Something you were so good at doing in high school."

"I didn't mean anything by it, Mia." His sharp glare drilled into her eyes. "As far as I'm concerned, that's in the past."

"Easy for you to say. You weren't the one wronged."

His eyes creased, and he ran a hand around the back of his neck. "Look—I'll admit I was hard on you back then. I should have been more understanding, what with the loss of your mom and all. But when you and Ryan started dating and his grades took a nosedive, I had to make you see what you were doing to him."

"And you thought going behind my back and trying to break us up instead of talking to me was the right way to do that?"

He shrugged. "Might've used the wrong method, but I had the right motive."

"As David's friend I expected more from you. You knew how much losing our mother changed our lives." She sent him a penetrating stare.

"All I can say in my defense is at the time I thought you were totally out of control. Figured you'd soon be breaking the law." He sighed. "I couldn't let you take Ryan down with you."

Mia could appreciate Russ's concern for his brother, but he had worried in vain. Ryan pushed her out of his life the day she learned of his unfaithfulness. "As it turns out, that wasn't a problem, was it?"

Russ cleared his throat. "What say we put all of this behind us and get on with your statement?"

His offer to make amends was out of character for the guy she had known, but he could have changed. He could be one of the good guys now. She nodded, putting aside their past differences in honor of his profession.

He pulled out a notepad and pen. "Okay, so I need you to tell me exactly what happened today."

She didn't want to recount the fire. The searing flames. Suffocating smoke. Terrifying emotions. But she had to comply. She launched into the story, skipping the warning at the post office and replaying the rescue of Jessie with concise comments devoid of the emotions still tumbling through her body.

"I'm sure by now you've heard Jessie saw a man start the fire." Mental exhaustion over telling the story made her tone fall off at the end.

"So," he leaned closer, his eyes filled with interest, "now that you've had time to think about the fire, do you have any ideas about who would want to do this?"

Ideas? Like her father was probably behind it? A fact she wasn't ready to share. "Not really."

"Not really, or no?"

She wasn't ready to tell him everything. She shrugged and tried to veil her eyes so he didn't notice her evasiveness. She'd had years of practice in subterfuge with her father, but that had been so long ago she'd forgotten how to do it.

Russ drew in air through his nose and held it while looking at the ceiling. Letting out the breath, he fixed a stern look on her face. "I get the feeling you're keeping something from me, Mia. It would be easier on both of us if you'd cooperate."

She'd cooperate as far as she could and still keep this in the family. When she got out of here, she'd confront her father and put an end to the mess. Then Russ wouldn't have anything to investigate.

She nodded solemnly as if she were taking his advice. "I'll spend some time thinking about who might have started the fire and get back to you." She held his gaze until a knock sounded on the door, and he turned to face it.

Mia eased out a breath of relief and watched as Ryan entered. Still dressed in his firefighting pants, the suspenders hanging limp, he strolled into the space with a confident smile. He let his gaze rove over her then linger on her face, warming her with the concern displayed in his eyes.

"Hope I'm not interrupting," he said half-heartedly.

Russ's foot hit the floor with a thud that echoed through the room, and Mia expected him to object to the interruption.

"Actually, you can help me out here," he said. "I was just about to share arson statistics with Mia. Specifically, that it's often committed by a property owner wanting to collect insurance money. With your training as a firefighter you can confirm that."

"Well, yeah…" Ryan crossed the room, regarding his brother with a skeptical look, "but if you're intimating Mia torched the barn for insurance money, you're way off base."

"Are you sure about that?"

"Positive." Support for Mia was etched on Ryan's rugged face.

Mia smiled her thanks and turned to Russ to see his reaction. His frozen features said it all. He believed she was involved in setting the fire.

His hand drifted to the top of his gun as if he were thinking he might need reinforcement. "On the surface it doesn't look like you'd benefit from the fire as the property would be worth more with the barn standing. But…" His eyes darkened and fixed on Mia's face like a mighty lion eyeing up lunch. "Maybe you can't wait that long for the cash. By destroying the barn, you'll get a nice settlement from the insurance company right away."

Her mouth fell open. "You're seriously considering me?"

"Got to check out all possibilities."

"You're wrong, bro," Ryan said.

Mia crossed her arms. "This is unbelievable. I'm almost killed in the fire and you suspect me of starting it. Guess you don't really believe your niece saw that man."

"Sure I do. You could've hired him."

"Right. I hired a man to burn the place down then got stuck in the barn."

"Accidents happen. You arranged to have the place torched but didn't know Jessie would be in there." He paused dramatically. "You couldn't let her die so you saved her. Got trapped. Wouldn't be the first time someone got caught in their own fire."

"Seriously, Russ, you're wasting time on me."

"Maybe. Maybe not."

Mia lurched forward and grasped the wooden arms of the chair. "But you—"

He held up his hand. "Don't worry. I'm not focusing solely on you."

"Good, then you'll find this guy and your case will be solved."

"Or maybe I'll find out you had a part in it. Trouble always found you in the past, Mia. Why would this be any different?"

Ryan shot out a hand and seared his brother with a heated look. "That was uncalled for. You should be thinking about how to protect Mia from the arsonist, not blaming her for the fire."

Russ stared at Ryan so long Mia thought the brothers might come to blows. Their behavior was so reminiscent of high school. Russ insisting Ryan break up with her. Ryan passionately defending her. The pair nearly duking it out before parting angry and hurt.

Without breaking eye contact, Russ slipped his notepad into his pocket, his movements deliberate and slow. "I appreciate your wanting to protect Mia, but you're overreacting. The fire wasn't about physically hurting her. If it had been, the arsonist would have made sure she was in the barn before setting the fire."

Ryan faced Mia. His withering stare made it clear that he wanted her to tell Russ about the threatening letter. She gave a quick shake of her head and hoped Russ didn't notice the interchange.

If he did, the controlled expression on his face didn't let on. "I apologize if my earlier comment crossed the line, Mia. I'm simply trying to locate the person behind this no matter who it is. The best thing you can do to clear your name right now is provide me with a copy of the will." Letting a pointed look pierce Ryan, Russ tromped out of the room.

"Excuse me," Ryan said and charged after his brother.

Watching him exit in hot pursuit of his brother, a wave of vulnerability crashed over her.

Was someone other than her father behind the fire and her life really in jeopardy? Had she done the right thing in keeping the letter from Russ…or had she left herself unprotected and in the path of a lunatic?

Ryan charged down the hallway, gaining on Russ who rushed away as if he hadn't done something so unbelievable. Mia was not guilty of arson and Ryan would not let Russ accuse her of it. How could he think Mia had anything to do with the fire?

Near the nurses' station, Ryan caught up to Russ and spun him around by the shoulder. "You're crazy, bro, if you think Mia was involved in this. She gains nothing until her year is over."

"Are you sure about that? Have you seen the will?" He paused and let his words linger in the air. "Maybe there's a loophole. Maybe she gets the cash now if insurance pays out."

Money never motivated Mia. She could have changed, but the warning letter pointed to someone else. If only he could tell Russ about the threat, Mia would be cleared. But Ryan promised.

He clenched his fist and let his fingernails bite into the palm to keep from revealing the secret. "Mia had nothing to do with the fire. Nothing."

Russ raised a skeptical eyebrow. "You gonna make a habit of defending her again?"

"She doesn't need my defense. She's done nothing wrong."

A righteous look radiated from his eyes. "Then it's not a problem if I investigate her."

Ryan's hands itched to throttle him and wipe that pious look off his face, but that wouldn't help. He wouldn't give in to the temptation. "Go easy on her, bro. She risked her life to save your niece, who might have died if Mia hadn't been so brave."

Russ studied Ryan's face until he grew uncomfortable under the intense scrutiny and asked, "What?"

"It just seems kind of odd you're defending her like this when you cheated on her and hurt her more than my questioning ever could."

"You know I did that for her."

"Then why do you feel so guilty about it?" Russ locked gazes with Ryan. "And while you're at it, maybe you should ask if your guilt is keeping you from seeing her involvement in the arson."

Ryan started to protest, but he was too caught off-guard by the comment to formulate the words.

Russ clapped Ryan on the shoulder. "Don't worry—I'm not trying to railroad Mia. I'm keeping an open mind. She may well be innocent. If so, you can say I told you so all you want. All I ask is that you think about it before you rush to her defense without any evidence to support your position." He lifted his hand and saluted. "I'll catch you later."

He clomped down the hallway and Ryan watched as questions pummeled his brain. Had he jumped to defend her without any thought? Was he simply protecting her on instinct from their past relationship? Or was she really innocent and in danger from an unknown source?

She had changed so much physically maybe her personality had drastically changed, too. The woman he once knew may not even exist anymore.

There was only one way to find out. Spend time with her. He spun and headed back toward her door. Before going home and cleaning up, he'd convince her to work with Wilderness Ways. That way if Russ was wrong and someone was out to get her, Ryan would be right by her side.

FIVE

The next morning, weariness from a sleepless night oozed from Mia's bones as Nurse Karen settled the blanket over her legs and then stepped behind a modern cart holding a computer.

"Once I finish this paperwork, you can get dressed and we'll get you out of here in no time." Humming quietly as if she loved her job, she input data into Mia's file.

Mia smiled over the lilting melody. Her mom used to sing this same song when she was happy. Mia closed her eyes and urged her muscles to relax. The notes rushed up the scale and plunged down bringing with them the last good memory Mia had of her mother.

Mia could almost feel the warm breeze skipping off the lake and into their cabin at Pinetree. Their family had just arrived for a much-needed vacation and her mom's face lit with happiness for the first time in months. Her parents didn't think she and David knew they fought over their father's neglect of the family for his job. But their vacation was supposed to fix all of that.

They had no sooner unpacked when her father pulled out his laptop and sat at the worn kitchen table to work on a medical book he was writing. Mia's joy evaporated along with her mother's. She issued an ultimatum. If Mia's father spent his days at Pinetree working on the book, the marriage was over.

Mia couldn't stand by and do nothing. She begged her father to take them for a ride in the country. He agreed and she was thrilled. She'd kept their parents together. Until she pointed out a deer coming from the woods and her father took his eyes off the road long enough for the car to slip onto the steep shoulder. He tried to wrestle the car back onto the pavement, but lost control and they slammed into a monster pine tree killing her mother instantly.

Mia sighed. Life would have been so much easier if God had let her mother live. If her father never blamed her for the accident. She'd blamed herself until counseling helped her see the futility of misguided guilt. Now she was able to enjoy thoughts of her mother.

Not so with Ryan and her father. She'd tried to let go of the drama with them as easily. But she'd dated too many men who reminded her of her controlling father to let go of the pain and bitterness.

A knock sounded on the door and Karen's humming ended.

Mia clung to the memories of her mom but they

drifted away with the music. Expecting Ryan, who'd offered to give her a ride home today, she opened her eyes and looked at the door.

Not Ryan. Her father.

His alert eyes searched the space and took in her appearance before creasing in a critical assessment and focusing on the computer.

She drew in a quick breath and held it.

"Doctor," Karen said, a hint of awe settling into her tone.

"I'll just have a quick peek at Mia's records." The raspy, yet firm voice instantly transported Mia back ten years.

Head bent low over the cart, the sound of his fingers clicking on the keyboard pinged through the room. Mia stared at a large void on the back of his head replacing thick black hair that had once thrived like shag carpeting. He didn't seem so intimidating anymore. More fragile and old. She eased out her breath. She could do this…

As if he sensed her perusal, he looked up. "Everything looks good, Mia," he said waving a hand over the computer. "You should make a full recovery."

This was so like him to put up the facade of being a concerned father in front of others. She couldn't stomach the two-faced behavior in high school and had rebelled against it, but after yesterday's stress, she didn't have the strength to fight him. Besides, if she was going to get him to confess his part in the fire, she'd better not embarrass him in front of Karen.

Mia smiled tightly. "I appreciate your taking the time to stop in. Do you have a few more minutes to talk?"

Pure astonishment took hold of his face. She hadn't responded positively to him in years. He didn't know what to make of this sudden about-face, and she didn't know what to say. An awkward silence descended on the room.

Karen cleared her throat. "If you're finished with the computer, Doctor, I'll get out of here so the two of you can catch up."

"Yes, of course," he said with a kind smile reserved for those who met his exacting standards.

As Karen departed, Mia grappled with what to do. She wanted to say something to keep him looking open and receptive, but when the nurse exited the room his door of kindness snapped shut, and his hard shell returned.

He picked a piece of dark lint off his white coat and flicked it into the air. "What is it you want, Mia?"

She felt like he'd just flicked her away as easily as the fuzz. Tears dampened her eyes but like so many times in the past, she willed them back and located her armor. She slipped inside the steel plating and drew a deep breath before firing her accusation.

"I received an interesting letter in the mail warning me to keep away from Pinetree or I would pay."

She fixed her gaze on his steely gray eyes. "I immediately recognized it as something you would do, but I never thought you'd want me out of here so badly you'd hire someone to burn down the barn."

He studied her, his eyes blank and unreadable. After a few painful moments, right when she was ready to squirm out from under his microscopic intensity, he heaved a sigh.

"As usual, you've made it very clear what you think of me. I won't respond to your accusation." He spun and exited the room.

What? He left. Just like that. He couldn't even be bothered to answer her. But why was she surprised? This was exactly what she'd expected from him. But not what she'd hoped he'd do.

Her lips quivered. Tears trickled out.

Even after years of his rejection, she'd hoped he'd deny the charges and declare he'd never hurt the daughter he loved and welcome her back. After all, that's what Uncle Wally had wanted when he structured his will to bring her back here for a year before inheriting Pinetree…and his plan had given her hope of the reconciliation. Her father didn't appear to have the same goal in mind.

No, with Uncle Wally dead, she was all alone and the finality of her loss swept through her like never before.

Ryan walked down the hospital hallway. He'd been surprised yesterday when Mia agreed to let him pick her up this morning and drive her home. Not that he should read anything into it. She likely agreed because Logan Lake had no public transportation and he was her only way out of this place. On the bright side, she was willing to take under consideration his request to fill in as a counselor at Wilderness Ways.

With the students arriving tomorrow, he hoped for a firm commitment from her. The last thing she needed with everything going on in her life was pressure from him, but he wasn't opposed to encouraging her to accept. Turning her focus on to the students could be just the thing to help take her mind off her problems.

He rounded the corner and spotted Mia's father exiting her room. Lips puckered, he slammed his hands into the pockets of his white coat and rushed down the hall. He didn't appear so much angry as dejected.

This was a good sign. Conversations between Mia and her father had always escalated into fights so boisterous it was a wonder they didn't end in violence. If the same thing had happened today, he'd have been fuming and storming away.

At the open door, the sound of crying surprised him and pulled him into the room. Mia lay back on the raised bed, her moist eyes as vulnerable as little Jessie's had been when he'd left her with the EMTs. The large gashes on Mia's cheek taped closed with butterfly bandages kicked him in the gut again.

He'd thought she'd look better this morning but her appearance was as delicate as fine china.

What could have happened to upset her this much, yet not affect her father the same way?

Ryan hated to bring it up, but if she needed to talk about the conversation, he would be more than willing to listen. "Mia, are you all right?"

Her eyes opened wider letting a wave of misery wash out. "Thanks for coming to get me, but I'm not ready to leave," she said between sobs. "The nurse still has to do the paperwork."

He'd witnessed hundreds of fights with her dad after she'd rebelled against his wishes, but the pain reflected in her eyes topped all of them. He couldn't stand by without offering comfort.

He crossed the room and sat next her. Careful not to tangle the IV and oxygen tubes, he drew her into his arms. She didn't resist but snuggled close, and her crying intensified.

"Shh." He rocked her and breathed in her scent, a combination of tart hospital soap and caustic smoke with a slight hint of her sweet perfume. Her body shook from her sobs and she clutched the back of his shirt as his shoulder grew damp from her tears.

If he could get a hold of her father right now, the man would pay. Something Ryan always wanted to do in high school, but was too young to act on. Her father had broken her heart so many times and Ryan picked up the pieces, restored her confidence and tried to prove she was loveable, but he'd never gotten the satisfaction of seeing her father suffer for hurting her.

And if Ryan lived the faith he professed, he'd forgive the man for the way he treated his daughter, and should also be thinking about how to help repair the rift between them.

She trembled and snuffled, winding down in her crying.

He hated that she was hurting, but he had to admit holding her again felt right. He would be happy to stay like this. Minus her crying, of course.

No. Not a good idea. He'd never make that kind of commitment to a woman again. Especially one who might be stepping into danger without any regard for her life.

He gently released her, located tissues on the table by the bed and offered them. "What did he say this time?"

"My father? You saw him?" Watery eyes fixed on his as she ripped out a tissue.

Ryan nodded.

"I told him about the letter and that I believed he was behind the fire." She hiccupped and dabbed at her red-rimmed eyes. "He didn't deny it."

Not as bad as Ryan had imagined from her over-the-top reaction. "He didn't admit to doing anything. That's a good thing, isn't it?"

"No! Even if he didn't do it," she sniffed, "he clearly wants nothing to do with me."

So this is what set her off. Not her father's guilt,

but his rejection. This wasn't a topic they could resolve in a short conversation, and Ryan didn't think he could offer anything new after all these years. He could sidestep the rejection and focus on the fire. Then maybe she'd be open to telling Russ about the letter and look for other suspects.

Ryan shifted on the edge of the bed. "Sounds to me like you really don't believe your father's behind all of this."

She blew her nose and set the tissue on her lap. "I don't know what to think anymore. I can't imagine he'd hire an arsonist, but he's the most logical candidate."

She was right. There was no other obvious suspect, but Ryan had to plant doubt in her mind to get her moving forward. "Think about it, Mia. Would your father really commit a criminal act and risk going to jail just to get you to leave town?"

She pulled out another tissue. "I know it doesn't make sense, but who else would've done it? David is the only one who would benefit if I left."

"In my opinion he's a less likely suspect than your father. He's as close to a model citizen as they come. Plus he seems to be doing well financially."

"I agree and that's why the more I think about him the more I rule him out." She sighed and twisted the tissue in her fingers. "It has to be my father."

Her agonizing expression left Ryan feeling helpless. He had no idea how to figure out the identity of the arsonist but he could offer his support.

He clasped her hand. "No matter who did this, I'm here to help you through it."

Her eyes lingered on his face. "You've been nothing but kind to me since I've gotten here." She released a shuddering breath. "I'm thankful for everything you've done. Saving me at the barn and all. Really, I am. Not that you could tell. All I've done is repay you with harsh words."

"I hurt you. I deserve your anger."

She worked her lower lip and went silent for so long he thought she might have changed her mind about engaging in this conversation. "Do you want to talk about it?"

"Now?"

She nodded. "I can't leave until the nurse discharges me. We might as well make good use of the time."

This was what he wanted, but now that it was time to talk, he didn't have a clue how to start. He'd always hoped she'd forgive him, but she might not. What if she didn't? What happened then?

"Ryan?" she said softly, and offered a nod of encouragement.

"Right, high school." He shifted on the bed. "So if we hadn't broken up that night what do you think would've happened between us?"

Her eyes widened.

He'd caught her by surprise. "This isn't a test or anything to see how you felt. Just a question."

"Well, you'd already started college. My grades

weren't good enough to get into Reed, so I would have gone to a community college or gotten a job so we could live close to each other."

He'd thought along the same lines. "And then… when I graduated, we'd get married and live happily ever after here in Logan Lake, right?"

"Something like that."

"And that's why I arranged for you to find me kissing Sheila and made you think I had something going on with her." He clamped his hand on the back of his neck and looked down to hide his embarrassment over the dumb decision he was about to explain. "You were so unhappy under your father's control. It was getting worse by the day. You wanted out of here more than anything except being with me." He looked up to gauge her reaction.

She met his gaze with clear green eyes that encouraged him to continue.

"I couldn't let you stay here and live under your father's thumb. You had to go out in the world and find out who you were without your father harping at you for everything. If you knew I wanted to spend the rest of my life with you, you would have settled here." He sighed heavily. "But if I made you think I didn't want to be with you anymore you'd run to Wally in Atlanta, which is exactly what you did."

He prayed for understanding. "And look at you. My gosh, just look at you. You're not working in some dead-end job with three kids and a loathing for your husband because he kept you here. You came back here strong and independent. Able to stand up to your father. A professional counselor respected by your peers."

She sat unmoving, her eyes fixed on his face. Tears began to slide down her cheeks. He didn't know how to respond. Were these tears of forgiveness or tears of loss? He reached out a thumb and swiped them away.

When she didn't pull away, a nervous laugh escaped his throat. "And now this is the part where you forgive me for hurting you because you realize I did what I did because I loved you."

She sniffed and ever so slightly nodded. "You had a good reason, and for that I can forgive you. But that doesn't erase the hurt. It'll take time for me to forget how it felt."

He reached out to take her in his arms but let his hands fall. He wanted to hold her until her tears stopped again, but he couldn't.

He wouldn't risk reconnecting as they had in high school. Couldn't risk caring for her again. She'd nearly died and this nightmare wasn't over. She was still in danger. If the man who set fire to the barn wanted to hurt her, Ryan wasn't sure he could stop him. Loss of Cara had proven his limitations.

SIX

Wishing she'd known about the condition of Ryan's truck before she accepted a ride, Mia sat back as they rumbled down the winding country road to the rattling of soda cans on the floor. Flies had succumbed to the quicksand of dust and grime on the dashboard, and cracks populated the seat with tufts of stuffing eager to escape. Redressed in her fire-ravaged clothes, Mia matched the interior, but not Ryan.

Today he wore an emerald shirt highlighting his dark coloring, and coordinating perfectly with heavy brown corduroys and rough hiking boots. He had a day's or more worth of stubble on his lean face, and as he climbed into the truck, a hesitant, little-boy-lost look had crossed his face and made it hard to keep her eyes off him.

Or was it the fact that he'd had a sound explanation for hurting her, and she'd finally forgiven him? But would she ever let go of the pain of his betrayal and learn to trust a man again? Was Ryan what he seemed or did he really have his own agenda—wanting to take over her life and control her?

Last night as she tried to fall asleep in the noisy hospital, her thoughts kept drifting back to the ambulance ride and his loving expression as he answered Jessie's questions and calmed her fears, much as he'd comforted her after her father's many rampages. Then she had to go and dream about Ryan.

Not just him, but them as a couple again, married and with a family. The whole American dream wrapped up in a neat little package. Two children, living in the big lodge at Pinetree, and of course a dog frolicking around the place. Foolish, but she liked it.

She glanced at his strong profile. How could she spend day after day working alongside him and not wonder what their life would have been like if they'd never broken up?

He slowed the truck at Pinetree's driveway and glanced her way. "You thinking about the fire again?"

She wasn't about to admit the truth so she lifted her shoulders in a shrug.

He seemed to buy her vague response as an affirmation and clicked on the blinker. "I don't have to tell you people who survive an experience like a fire often start to ponder the meaning of life and why they were spared. I'm not sure how you stand on God these days, but He can help you through this if you turn to Him."

She swiveled toward Ryan so fast her hair slapped her face. "You've embraced religion?"

His lips tipped in the briefest of smiles. "I turned my life over to God a few years ago if that's what you mean."

She peered past him and out the window. Here she was fantasizing over getting back together with him, and he clearly wasn't the same person she'd known in high school. Back then, he'd have scoffed at anything religious. Now he was spouting the stuff.

"Mia." He laid a calloused hand on her arm. "Would you mind if I tell you how my faith helped me get through some tough times?"

She shook her head. "That's the last thing I need right now. God keeps taking away the people I love most, and I haven't the stomach to think about Him."

"That's not how it is, Mi—"

"I said no to this sermon, all right?" She sent a stony gaze his way.

He responded with a flush of hurt, but she kept quiet.

Religion or God or whatever Ryan wanted to call things did not help her. She'd tried that. Until her mom died and her father ignored her. Then God ceased to exist.

Out of the corner of her eye, she saw Ryan blow out a deep breath. His knuckles tightened on the wheel, turning white then slowly returning to healthy pink.

Something inside her begged to comfort him, to take back her comment, to reach out and touch his arm to end the silence. To return the carefree guy from before this conversation, but she held herself in check and gazed out the side window. No good would come from revisiting her stance on God.

Ryan set aside the rebuff and replaced it with the resolve to try again later. Mia believed in God. At least enough to blame Him for the loss of her mother. This meant Ryan had a chance of helping her let go of that blame and perhaps moving her toward God again. But now was not the right time.

Now he'd let her see that as a Christian he wouldn't take her rejection personally.

"So," he said, putting a cheerful tone into his words. "Did you have a chance to think about helping us at Wilderness Ways?"

She arched a perfectly plucked brow. "I'm not sure it would be such a good match. I'm not much of an outdoor girl anymore. The thought of camping for days without a shower makes me cringe."

Her reaction didn't surprise him. After all, he'd have to be blind not to notice the change in her appearance to a real girly girl. But he was way ahead of her. Last night he'd thought of all the reasons she might say no and prepared a defense for each one of them. She didn't stand a chance.

"Actually," he paused and turned a high wattage smile on her, "I rethought this last night. It wouldn't be wise to send you into the field with students. With the injuries you suffered, I'm not sure you're up to the physical demands this kind of trip could place on you."

Her eyes narrowed. "So why ask if I wanted to help?"

"I have another plan for you." With his free hand, he pretended to twist a handlebar mustache like a villain.

She laughed as she always had when he'd worked hard to brighten up her mood. "And what plan might that be?"

"I'll shift staff so you can work with the students at the base camp. We start each session with initial evaluations at Pinetree when the students arrive. This provides the field staff with a risk assessment for each student. Then every week the students come in and we hold another round of counseling."

"You didn't have to resort to your dastardly villain routine to get me to agree. I would love to do that." A guarded expression captured her face. "But if I do, you have to agree to keep things between us on a professional level."

He refused to let her see the pain. "Whatever you need, Mia, I can do that."

"Good. Then I'm ready and willing to help."

He glanced at her and their eyes met. Her passion for helping others radiated in waves and warmed him far more than was good for him. They'd always shared a compassion for helping the underdog, and now they both made their living doing that very thing.

He returned his focus to the road. "It's amazing we both ended up in the same line of work."

"I wasn't at all surprised when I heard what you did for a living. You're a natural at it. Your support in high school was about the only thing that kept me going."

And he'd hurt her when he withdrew his support. But that was over now, thanks to her forgiveness. "I always knew you'd do something to help struggling teens, and I'm very glad you have the skills to help my program."

"So how long have you been working with Wilderness Ways?"

"I came back to Logan Lake about three years ago and took on the directorship a year and a half ago."

"Really. You didn't come back here after college?" She swiveled to face him.

He could feel her questioning eyes burning into his face. He had to keep his focus on the road so he didn't find himself telling her more than he could handle revealing right now.

"I went to grad school in Eugene and then stayed there to work at a small clinic." The same clinic Cara worked for. The clinic she died in. His chest tightened the way it always did at the memory of finding Cara on the floor of her office. The blood pooling around her. Her face pale. Her pulse barely there.

He sucked in a cleansing breath and gestured at

Pinetree's main entrance to direct Mia to the scenery and away from his face. "We're here."

Mia's perceptive face told him she saw right through his plan and would probably question him about this subject later. But at least he'd bought some time before he had to recount the day Cara's life ended at the hands of a crazed patient.

Mia let Ryan's evasive behavior pass. He obviously had something he didn't want to talk about and she had no desire to pry for fear of dredging up their own old wounds. She sat back and studied the scenery she'd not seen yesterday when she arrived through the other gate.

First they passed the resort's check-in hut only used during the peak summer season. Next came a grouping of worn cabins, the office/convenience store, and a large recreation center, all located near the beach at Logan Lake.

"Everything looks the same." The longing in her tone caught her off-guard. It quickly ended as the hull of the barn came into view and a wave of fear surged through her.

Ryan tipped his head at the barn. "When I got home last night, I brought your car up to the lodge and your luggage inside."

"Thank you." She let her voice ring with sincerity at his continued kindness. She was learning a lot about her old boyfriend and except for the religion thing, she liked what she saw. Liked it too much for her own good.

They made the last curve to approach the lodge. A police car, large black sedan, pickup truck and two SUVs lined up like dominoes in front of the lodge.

"What's going on?" she asked with rising concern. "Do you think something else's happened?"

"Now don't jump to conclusions and start worrying. There's likely an innocent explanation." He smiled at her but sped the truck faster.

Her stomach tightened at his reaction. Maybe something happened to Jessie. The man in the barn might have learned she could identify him, and he'd come after her.

Mia suddenly wished she believed God heard her prayers, as she would offer one for Jessie. But He didn't, so what was the point? He didn't spare her mother when she asked, so He wouldn't spare a child because she requested His help. Nor did He seem inclined to keep her out of harm's way.

Climbing from the truck, she took in the cane-backed rocking chairs and a massive swing cluttering the huge wraparound porch. She and Uncle Wally had spent hours sitting out here, and the enormity of his loss hit her hard.

"C'mon," Ryan said, coming up behind her. "I can hear them laughing inside. If something was wrong, they wouldn't be having such a good time." He must have thought her reluctance to enter was from fear of what waited for them inside.

The door flashed open and Jessie, who was tugging the leash of a small white dog with eyes circled in black like a little mask, raced down the stairs.

"Get control of him, Jessie." A man whose eye color identified him as a Morgan and whose parental tone identified him as Reid, lingered at the door.

Jessie tightened the leash and barreled into Mia surrounding her waist in a tight hug.

Mia lurched back in pain but regained her composure and smiled down on Jessie. The innocent fragrance of baby shampoo enveloped her head like a halo. Tears of gratitude for being able to save this precious child's life threatened to fall.

Mia scrunched her eyes and hugged harder. "I'm so glad to see you're doing okay."

Jessie gazed up at Mia with hero worship she knew she didn't deserve. She was just in the right place at the right time. How could she possibly live under such high expectations?

The dog yipped in excitement giving Mia the chance to turn the focus in another direction. She bent over and cupped the dog's head. "Hey, little fella."

He ran his pink tongue over her palm, and she scooped him up. "Is he your dog, Jessie?"

"Kinda, but not really. Daddy won't let me have a dog. He says he doesn't have the time to take care of anyone but me." Her lower lip shot out, and she plopped down onto a step.

Jessie's pain hung in the air like the smoke from the barn had.

Were Jessie and Reid living the same life Mia had with her father? Mia lifted her head and looked up at Reid.

Ryan leaned forward and whispered, "I know what you're thinking, but it's nothing like what you went through. Jessie is oversimplifying things. Reid's a great father, but he's really struggling to cope and a dog is just too much right now."

Mia offered a clipped nod to let Ryan know she understood.

Reid came down the stairs and held his hand in greeting. "It's good to see you again, Mia. I'll never be able to repay you for saving Jessie." His voice caught, and he cleared his throat. "I hope you don't mind that we took over the lodge, but we wanted to bring a few friends over to say thanks."

Mia hid her surprise by focusing on Bandit and stroking her fingers down his back. "And does that include Bandit?"

Reid cast a concerned look at Jessie and shook his head. "We didn't know he'd be here."

Jessie popped up and pointed at Bandit's bandaged wrapped rear leg. "He got a bad 'fection on his leg and had to stay at Doc's for a really long time. Now he's all better so Doc brought him home."

Ryan stepped forward. "Bandit was Wally's dog. When Wally was up here in the summer to run the camp, Bandit lived in the lodge. When Wally went back home, Bandit stayed in the barn and Jessie took care of him."

"I took good care of him." Her eyes turned protective.

Ryan inched between Mia and Jessie. "Since Bandit no longer has a home in the barn, we were hoping you'd keep him with you at the lodge."

Jessie slipped around Ryan and looked up at Mia with hopeful eyes. "If you keep him, I can help you take care of him."

Jessie's anguish pierced Mia's heart. The poor child had been through so much. Mia had never had a dog and had no idea what owning one entailed, but it would be good for Jessie if she would keep the pup.

"What do you say, Bandit?" She cuddled him against her chest, his black-tipped tail thumped like a pendulum on her arm. "You want to live with me?" His tongue lapped her neck.

Still smiling, she looked at Ryan. "How about we try it for a few days to see how things go?"

"Yes." Jessie shot a fist into the air and danced around.

"Thank you," Reid mouthed.

Jessie grabbed Mia's hand and tugged. "C'mon. Let's go to the party."

"Not so fast, Jessie," Reid warned. "Mia needs to take things easy for a few days."

Mia smiled at Reid and put Bandit down. Jessie

grabbed the leash and pulled Mia with less force but her face continued to hold her enthusiasm.

Mia let herself be led into the lodge. She hadn't been inside for years so she paused in the entryway to look around. Heavy, rustic furniture filled the room. The same sturdy leather sofa angled in front of a massive stone fireplace was home to many long discussions with Uncle Wally. Same chunky coffee table made from old barn wood that had held game boards and cards. Same worn recliner hugged the corner.

Today, intimate groups of people mingled in the large space in a party kind of atmosphere. At least they had mingled, until one by one, eyes turned to focus on her. They continued to smile, belying an undercurrent surging through the air. People in Logan Lake had never seen her in a positive light due to her rebellious ways and they definitely never threw her a party. What in the world did they expect her to do?

From the far side of the room, Russ looked over the heads of a group and fixed assessing eyes in her direction.

Ryan must have felt her unease as he came forward and placed his hands on her shoulders. He gave a comforting squeeze and looking down, he searched her eyes. She let herself linger for a moment in the depth of his caring before giving a clipped nod to let him know she was okay.

"Move over, Uncle Ryan." Jessie's lips morphed into a sweet little pout. "You're hogging Mia."

He ruffled Jessie's hair. "Don't worry, Squirt, I'll share her with you."

"C'mon, Mia." Jessie tugged harder on Mia's hand. "There's a present on the table for you. I can help you open it…if you need me to." Jessie pointed toward a box covered in multicolored balloon paper sitting on the coffee table. "See?"

Mia moved a few feet. As the people gathered around watching her with expectancy, her steps faltered. She'd often fantasized about overcoming the negative reputation her teenage rebellion had fostered. But in those dreams never had she been dressed in burnt and torn clothes with scraggly hair hanging from her head.

She ran her free hand over the tangled locks. "You really didn't have to do this."

They glanced at one another in confusion. Embarrassed looks followed.

Reid laughed nervously. "Wish we *had* thought to get you something for all you did. We found the package on the porch when we got here."

Oh, no. They didn't bring the gift. She looked to Ryan for his reaction. His face lit with surprise, and he offered no assistance other than a gentle smile of support.

What did etiquette dictate in a situation like this? Should she open the package or ignore it? If she did open it, the focus would be on the gift and giver, not on her.

"C'mon, Mia." Jessie tugged harder making Mia's decision for her.

She made eye contact with her visitors and let her lips tip in a reticent smile. "I'll just see what this is." She dropped Jessie's hand and rushed to the package. "No card. Maybe the sender put a note inside."

"Can I help open it?" Jessie pleaded as she skidded to a stop at the table. Unable to stop as fast, Bandit slammed into Jessie's leg and looked dazed.

Mia smiled fondly at Jessie. "Why don't you pull off the paper?"

Jessie handed Bandit's leash to Reid and ripped the wrapping into shreds, tossing the fragments on the wide wooden floor planks. She put her hand on the box, and her eyes telegraphed her desire to pull up the flap.

"Jessie," Reid said with a warning tone. "This is Mia's present."

"That's okay," Mia said. "Go ahead."

Jessie started to lift one flap when a sheet of white paper slipped free and drifted to the floor.

"Hold on, sweetie," Mia said as she retrieved the paper. "Let's see who it's from before you open it."

A giggly Jessie danced in place as Mia began to unfold the paper.

The page held letters cut from a magazine, very similar to the warning she'd received in the post office. Her stomach twisted. She scanned the message.

Sever your claim to Pinetree or I'll sever it for you.

Jessie's hand reached for the flap.

"Don't!" Mia shouted. "Don't open it."

Jessie looked up. Her eyes were filled with surprise over Mia's harsh command, and her mouth was wide open and ready to wail. Bandit raised his head and frantically barked.

Mia eased between Jessie and the box. She clamped a hand on the lid then picked up the box and took it to the kitchen counter.

She opened and peered inside.

Oh, no!

She dropped the note into the box covering the horrible sight. Her stomach roiled. Acid burned. Nausea sent her bolting for the nearest bathroom.

On her knees near the claw-foot bathtub, she drew in a deep, cleansing breath and waited for her stomach to cease cramping.

Who could have done this? Her father? Did he hate her this much? Or was it someone else? And if so…why?

The image of the hand and note drilled into her mind.

One thing came across in screeching clarity. This perpetrator wanted her gone and was willing to go to extreme lengths to make it happen.

SEVEN

Ryan's chest had tightened at the sight of Mia's colorless face when she'd rushed past. He'd started to follow her until Russ clamped a hand on his arm and drew him toward the box. Russ picked up the note and held it open.

Sever your claim to Pinetree or I'll sever it for you.

Ryan turned from the warning similar to the note at the post office and looked into the box. At the sight of a severed hand lying on a bed of tissue paper, he slammed the lid.

Wait. Did he see right?

He looked again. The hand was rubber. Fake.

"She didn't hang around long enough to see this isn't real," Ryan whispered to Russ.

"Real or not we need to end this little party. Stay by the box until I clear the room," Russ said in a low voice, then clapped his hands together and turned to face the gawking guests. "Okay, folks. This party was probably not a good idea so soon after Mia got out of the hospital. She needs to get some rest so I suggest we all clear out."

His official police chief's voice stirred the guests to speculate on what happened but didn't move them out.

Ryan let his gaze travel to the hallway Mia had run down, and it was all he could do to stand guard over the box.

Father, please ease Mia's pain and help us catch the monster behind these threats.

"C'mon, people. Let's give Mia some privacy." Russ strolled through the family room and herded the guests toward the exit.

Holding a fearful Jessie in his arms, Reid caught his brother's gaze and made a call me sign with his finger and thumb, then exited. The minute the door closed behind the last guest, Ryan charged down the hall.

He knocked on the bathroom door. "Mia, the hand isn't real. It's just one of those fake rubber ones."

Silence. He could almost hear her thoughts. The same thoughts that weighed heavy on his mind. Fake hand or not, the person sending the letters made sure Mia knew he wouldn't hesitate to harm her if she didn't leave.

Mia was thankful Ryan told her the hand was fake. For the few minutes she'd believed it to be real, the terror engulfing her had been unbearable. Not that her fear had been totally erased. The letter conveyed the sender's intent to keep after her until she left, raising the ante if she refused to leave.

She stared at her reflection in the mirror for the second time in as many days. Who was this woman peering back at her? Was it her? Oh, the physical appearance with a few added scrapes and sutures was the same, but gone was the confident woman she'd become. Now an insecure tint haunted her face.

Well, no more.

She pushed back. She wouldn't let years of hard work disappear in less than two days. She'd put her insecurities behind her, take charge of her life again and find the person behind these threats. Nothing would deter her from doing her time here at Pinetree, and then returning to Atlanta to resume her real life.

In the family room, her heart skipped a beat as she passed the empty table where Jessie had been so excited about opening the brightly wrapped box. She forced her eyes from the fearful sight and on to Bandit, who lay on a plush bed in the corner. Across the room, Ryan leaned against maple cabinets in the kitchen, a phone to his ear. He waved her over.

She padded to the open kitchen where a wrought-iron pot rack swarming with worn copper and cast-iron cookware hung above a long island and separated the two rooms.

Ryan mouthed, "David."

Her new plan started by finding the person behind

these incidents, and getting David's take on things was near the top of her list.

"I need to talk to him," she answered.

Ryan clamped his palm on to the receiver. "Are you okay?"

She let her lips form into what she thought was a brave smile. "I'm fine."

His eyes said he didn't believe her. "Are you sure?"

"Positive."

He tilted his head in question then shook it and held up a finger before resuming his conversation.

She slipped on to a counter-height stool and watched bright rays filtering in from a picture window flicker on his wavy hair.

He looked up and flashed a hint of a smile at the sight of her watching him. He crossed to the island and held out the phone. "Your turn."

She reached for the handset. He pulled it against his chest and issued a playful dare.

Her eyebrows shot up. Had her forgiveness made him think she wanted to start something with him? If so, she'd end that notion when she got off the phone with David. If she was going to resume control over her life, she certainly wouldn't fall under the spell of a man. Especially *this* man.

Phone in hand, she turned away from him. "David."

"I was out of town and just heard about the fire."

He sounded concerned. "Ryan tells me you're doing okay."

"Ryan's right—I'm fine." She felt Ryan's eyes on her as he took the stool next to her, but she wouldn't look at him. "Do you have time to get together this afternoon?"

Over the phone, she heard papers rustling in the background. "Sorry, I've got appointments until late tonight. The soonest I can see you is eleven tomorrow morning. Could you stop by the office then?"

"I'll be there. Bye, David." She clicked off and reached across the island to hook the phone on the cradle.

Ryan leaned into her space. "You seem pretty calm after what just happened in here."

She swallowed the fear lodged deep inside her chest and shrugged. "I can't live afraid all the time like I've been doing since I got here. I have to take charge of my life again."

He rested his elbows on the counter, placing his head eye level with hers. "After what's happened I'd think you'd realize you can't control things."

Why did he have to say that and try to ruin her attempt at moving forward?

She crossed her arms to protect herself from the emotions simmering under the surface. "I have to admit it's been difficult lately. My life has been in turmoil since Wally died. I didn't want to come back here, but it was Wally's final request."

Ryan lifted his hand over hers but she pulled it

back before he could connect and undermine her determination.

She continued. "You know Uncle Wally was more of a father to me than my father so I had to honor him. Then these terrible things happened and for a while I let them take over." She paused and cast a confident gaze at Ryan. "But I refuse to live under the control of others any longer."

He searched her face for what seemed like an eternity, before straightening to full height. "That's what scares you the most, isn't it? Not the danger you're in, not your father's attitude, but that you've lost complete control of your life."

She didn't expect him to contest her determination. True, he might see this strength as her way of standing up to him, but he should be proud of her resilience.

She squared her shoulders. "You sound like there's something wrong with trying to plan."

"Planning is one thing, trying to control things is another." He fired back with a challenging stare. "You can have every minute of every day planned and bad things will still happen."

"Ha! Don't I know it, but if I have a plan to follow when bad things happen I can get back on track." She paused to catch a breath. "I can't afford to live any other way. I'm all alone in this world, Ryan. People either die or disappoint me." She couldn't stand to see the anguish shooting into his eyes so she bolted from her chair and went to the picture window overlooking the lake.

"Mia," his voice came from right behind her, sending a quick jolt into her body.

She wanted to face him, but she didn't want his piercing gaze to sway her. "I really have a lot to do, so I think you should go now."

"I can't leave you feeling this way." He gently turned her by the shoulders.

His touch burned her like heat from the barn fire and left her throat dry as she tried to tell him to back off.

She started to move away, but he tightened his hold and rested his forehead on hers. "You don't have to be so tough all the time. You're not alone. I'm here to help you through this."

She breathed the musky sweet scent of his cologne and slowly exhaled. What could she say with him this close? Too close. Even if she could form the words, her mind couldn't form a coherent thought other than what would happen if he kissed her?

What a fool she was. Someone was going to great lengths to chase her away, her father still hated her and all she could think of was kissing the man who betrayed her. She pulled back.

"Mia, don't. Let me help." He reached up to cup the uninjured side of her face.

She peered into his eyes and saw the hope and healing waiting for her if she could only let go of the past. "I wish I could trust you."

He drew in a breath and seemed to withdraw mentally as he physically stepped back. He glanced around as if looking for a way to change her mind. He was wasting his time. She'd gained control again, and she wouldn't let him back in. She crossed her arms.

He went to the island and picked up a manila folder.

"This is Eddie Kramer's file. He's the student I told you about yesterday." Ryan forced the heavy folder into her hands. "If you can fit him into this new life you're planning, take a look at the file. I'll be at the rec center all afternoon, and I'd appreciate it if you'd stop by for a short orientation on our procedures."

Ryan plodded out the door and down the stairs. Her heart tightened and the urge to run after him nearly had her feet moving, but she hadn't worked so hard to build a life for herself to toss it away on a whim.

No. She was back in control and ready to put her plan into action.

Ryan stormed down the steps and hopped into his truck. Mia was officially the most stubborn woman on earth. She'd erected the wall she was so famous for putting up when trouble threatened. A tall wall. An unscalable wall. One he'd never been on the wrong side of before and he didn't know how—or even if he wanted to try—to bring it down.

He shoved the key into the ignition and backed the truck around. On the driveway, he spotted Russ's car and a tow truck at the barn. He'd not said anything about the truck or who owned it.

After Mia's latest rejection, Ryan had half a mind to go straight to the rec center and let her fend for herself. After all, she'd made it perfectly clear that she didn't need his help. However, after a moment's indecision he groaned and swung the wheels left toward the barn. This didn't mean he was helping Mia. He was just curious. That was all.

At the barn, he hopped out and approached Russ who leaned over the hood of his car and filled out a form attached to a clipboard.

"You ID the owner yet?"

Russ looked up in surprise. "If you're down here that must mean Mia came out of her hiding hole. She doing okay?"

Ryan's turn to be surprised at his brother's concerned tone.

"Fine." The answer came out too curt not to clue Russ into his frustration.

Russ ripped off the top page on the pad and glared at Ryan. "I won't ask what put you in that mood."

Ryan looked away from the intense stare and watched the tow-truck driver secure the chains. "You never said if you found out who owns the truck."

"Not yet. Whoever boosted it was smart enough to remove VIN numbers. Likely a pro."

"And that makes him a pro? The average Joe knows enough to take that little tag off the dashboard."

"Yeah, but what the average Joe doesn't know is the number is etched on various parts of the vehicle." He tipped his head at the tow-truck driver securing chains on the truck. "Bobby here just told me the arsonist filed off all of them."

Ryan looked at Bobby and the destroyed truck. He swung his head back toward Russ and caught sight of the package Mia received sitting on the front seat of Russ's patrol car. If the man was a professional at stealing trucks, had no qualms about torching the barn and sent a message like the one in that box, what was he capable of doing to Mia if she didn't comply with his demands?

EIGHT

Mia closed Eddie's folder and laid it on the table next to the sofa. The teen's story dredged up memories of her own painful past and steeled her resolve to help him. Even if it meant spending every day with Ryan. No cost was too great to keep Eddie from ruining his life more than he had already. He'd been a model student until his parents died in a car crash. He'd bounced from foster home to foster home for the last three years and had a rap sheet filled with misdemeanor offenses.

She could certainly identify. She'd never been arrested and wasn't an orphan, but the way her dad treated her, she often felt as if she was all alone in the world. And if her father was behind the threats, she might as well be an orphan.

She would head to the rec center for the orientation on Wilderness Ways procedures Ryan suggested then check in with Verna Swann, Pinetree's manager, about filing an insurance claim and get her take on the fire.

"Here, boy," Mia rose and called Bandit.

He hopped up from the fuzzy bed in the corner by the fireplace and charged across the room.

"I'm so glad to have you." She snuggled him tight and laid her cheek against his soft head. "I need a friend who doesn't try to control my every move."

She walked past the counter where the box had last sat and was now replaced by her purse. In preparation for her trip to the resort office, she'd retrieved Uncle Wally's will and shoved it next to the warning letter from yesterday.

Today's warning along with a vision of the severed hand pierced her mind. A quick shiver rippled over her.

The stakes had been raised. Ryan was right. She had to give the first letter to Russ, but she didn't have to tell him she suspected her father. When she got to the office, she'd make a copy in case she needed it after she handed the original over to Russ.

"You can also be my watchdog." She gave Bandit one last hug and settled him into his crate. "Keep me safe."

Outside, she jogged down the steps and followed the path toward the garage. Fall days could start out chilly like today had, but the late afternoon sun broke through puffy clouds warming her back. Taking back her life and taking charge again felt good.

She entered the garage through the side door. The green John Deere utility vehicle sat in the only clean spot of the garage, keys dangling from the ignition.

Leave it to Wally not to lock the door and leave keys in vehicles. He was so trusting.

"Duh!" She slapped a palm against her head. "That's it."

Wally didn't lock anything. So why was the barn locked yesterday? Not with a simple little padlock but a massive chain. She never thought to ask Ryan if the south end was chained, too, but if it was, how did the arsonist get in? Did he have a key, or cut the chain? Maybe Verna could shed light on this, too.

Mia's excitement grew as she cranked the engine. After a few false starts, the cart sputtered out of the garage and putt-putted down the twisting drive. At the rec center, she pulled open the door. She heard conversation so she tiptoed in and lingered behind the bleachers to see what was going on.

Ryan sat at the head of a long table filled with his staff members who discussed the upcoming arrival of the students. She'd taken too long to get ready and now he was busy. She wouldn't interrupt but would come back after checking in with Verna.

She turned to go, but something pulled her back. She studied Ryan and the devotion for these students displayed in his tone and on his face. His students were fortunate to have him as their advocate. A feeling she knew from when he was her protector. Since Wally died, she had no one by her side. Maybe she should let go of her hurt and let Ryan fill that role again.

She shook her head and walked to the door. That

was just crazy thinking. She'd rather be on her own than risk losing control and trusting him again.

Ryan checked the cage-covered clock from his seat at the head of a long table surrounded by his staff. Through two hours of status updates, he'd had to force himself to keep his mind off Mia and on his hard-working staff members.

For the first hour, he'd actually hoped she'd stop in for orientation on her duties as a counselor, but when the clock neared the second hour, he gave up. Maybe after their conversation she'd decided she couldn't work with him. When Ian finished his report, the staff meeting would end and Ryan would be free to check in with her.

"Did you hear me, Ryan?" Ian asked, a bit of irritation in his tone.

"Sorry, what did you say?"

"I asked if you think the fire and that bizarre incident at the lodge this morning will have any impact on our program."

Ryan wasn't surprised at the question. Gossip spread fast in a small town and his staff members weren't immune. "We always keep the students in eyesight anyway, so I wouldn't worry about them any more than we usually do."

His phone chimed. He looked at caller ID—Russ.

"Sorry," he said to his staff. "I've got to get this. Let's take a quick break."

"Hey, bro." Ryan kept his tone purposefully light to make up for their terse words earlier.

"Do you remember Mia ever having a charm bracelet?" He snapped out each word forcefully like bullets shooting into the phone.

A charm bracelet? "That's the oddest question you've ever asked me. Why do you want to know about a bracelet?"

"Just answer the question."

Ryan had about enough of Russ's attitude, but a decisiveness in his tone said he was on to something important. Something that might not be in Mia's favor. She couldn't handle another tragedy right now.

He ran through the hours they'd spent together. The only time he remembered her out of torn jeans or cut-offs and T-shirts was when they went to prom. And the only thing on her wrist that night was the orchid corsage from him. "I remember crazy earrings but no bracelets."

"I'm talking about the kind of bracelet she might not wear but keep in her jewelry box. Girls collect charms from special events and put them on a chain." His tone said he had no understanding of why girls might do this.

"Sorry, bro, don't remember anything like that."

"When's her birthday?"

"October 15th. Why?"

"I took the rubber hand back to the office for processing. The tech found a bracelet stuck in the tissue paper. Looks like whoever sent the package tried to strap the bracelet on the wrist, but it dropped into the tissue. It has a birthday cake charm with October 15 engraved on it. It also has several charms from the Atlanta area Mia might have collected. All were dated before her mom died."

An uneasy feeling settled into Ryan's stomach. If she owned such a special memory of her mom, Ryan would have seen it. "This can't be Mia's bracelet. I would've known if she had one."

"Maybe you don't know as much about her as you think."

Ryan might be on her short list of people to avoid right now, but he knew her as well as anyone could. At least he used to, but now he couldn't be sure. "I don't think it's hers."

"Well, we'll soon find out. I'm leaving my office right now to confirm it with her."

Then she'd need Ryan by her side whether she thought so or not. "I'll meet you at the lodge."

"This is official business. You need to keep out of it."

Ryan disconnected before Russ made him promise not to come. He would be with Mia when Russ asked her about the bracelet. Even with her recent rejection, no way he'd let her go through another interrogation by Russ all alone.

In the John Deere, Mia crested a hill leading down to the lake. She let the vehicle coast to the bottom and swung into the space next to a small gold Honda parked out front of the office. Good, this must be Verna's car.

Once inside, Mia looked for Verna.

"Mia...Mia...is that really you?" A high and flighty voice, not at all like Verna's gruff smoker's tone, called from behind the door.

Mia pressed the door all the way open.

A young woman jogged around a small secretary's desk. She'd topped khaki pants with a white blouse and finished off the conservative outfit with a pair of leather boots Mia would kill to own. She knew Mia, but her identity was a mystery.

"Oh, my goodness, it *is* you," she said when she reached Mia. "I heard you were back but I refused to believe it until I laid eyes on you."

Mia returned the perky blonde's infectious smile. "Do I know you?"

"Sydney...Sydney Tucker."

Tucker? Mia knew the name, but the Tuckers in Logan Lake multiplied faster than bunnies. She could belong to one of any number of families.

"Clueless, huh?" She giggled like a devious child. "I'm Adam's cousin from Portland."

Mia's eyes flew open at the name of her high school friend. "But you're so...so..."

"Normal-looking?" She tossed back her head and laughed. "Gave up the piercings after high school. The shock value no longer got what I wanted."

"I would never in a million years have guessed your identity."

Sydney mocked a runway pose. "I'll take that as a compliment."

"And now you work here?"

She nodded. "I suppose you're here to see Verna."

"I am. Is she around?"

"Nah. Lucky for you the warden is taking a long lunch again today."

A warden? Not the Verna that Mia recalled. Maybe things changed around here more than she had first thought. "I remember her as being so sweet."

"I wish." Sydney perched on the corner of her cluttered desk. "Things were cool around here until Wally died. Now every little thing sends her ballistic."

Mia's radar beeped at full alert. Why would Verna's attitude change when Wally died? Mia had always thought Verna was close to Uncle Wally, but her outlook didn't sound like grief over his passing. So what then?

The door flew open with a crash against the wall. Mia spun around.

Verna, carrying a large bag of office supplies in one hand and a travel mug in the other trudged into the office. She eyed Sydney with a stern reprimand. "Come get this shredder. If you have time to sit around and gossip you have time to help me clean up this place."

Sydney passed Mia, giving her an I-told-you-so look on the way.

Mia followed Sydney. "Hi, Verna. It's good to see you."

Verna let her purse slide down her arm and plop on to the desk. "About time you decided to stop in, Mia."

Ohh, she *was* testy. That wouldn't deter Mia from asking about the barn, but she'd ease into it.

Mia pulled the will from her purse and held it up. "I was wondering if I could make a copy of this."

Verna jabbed a finger at the far wall. "Over there in the corner."

"Thanks," Mia said as she crossed the room and started copying. "So, Verna," Mia said keeping her tone casual and her gaze neutral, "I was wondering when you started locking the barn?"

Verna's penciled-in eyebrows arched. "We never lock the barn."

"The doors were chained on the day of the fire."

"That's news to me." She slowly laced her fingers together and stared at them in fascination.

"So, any idea of who might have locked it?"

Her gaze darted around the room then lighted on a pack of Lucky Strikes that had fallen from her purse. She tapped out a cigarette and dangled it from the corner of her mouth. "Nothing in there worth locking up." She dropped onto a sagging chair. "Now if you don't mind, I have work to do."

That was the best non-answer Mia had ever heard.

Verna might be hiding something, but her face turned hard and closed, telling Mia pushing harder for answers would only spook the woman. She'd have to come back later and better ease into the topic.

Mia put the will and copy into her purse. "One more thing before I go. Did Uncle Wally handle the insurance on the property or did you?"

Verna dug in her purse and extracted a blue lighter. "Wally didn't handle much of anything."

"So have you filed a claim for the barn, then?"

"The fire was just yesterday. I ain't no miracle worker." The cigarette bobbed with each word.

"Do you think you can get to it today?" Mia replaced the will with the letter, making sure to hide the large letters from Verna and Sydney's view.

"Like I said, I ain't a miracle worker."

"I can file the claim," Sydney said, her voice lighting with joy over irritating Verna.

"No. You've got things to do already. I'll make time for it."

"I'll check back tomorrow to see if there's anything you need from me." Mia smiled at Verna and turned to the door. She mouthed thank you to Sydney and waved.

Mia climbed into the John Deere and stared at the office. This was an interesting development. Verna wouldn't inherit Pinetree under any circumstance, but she was acting weird enough to earn a place on Mia's suspect list.

NINE

The steep incline on the drive from the rec center had forced Ryan to keep his speed down. He was just making the last curve when he spotted Russ's squad car parked near the garage. Ryan had hoped to arrive at the lodge before Russ, but at least the trip had given him time to pray for a positive outcome and prepare for the inevitable confrontation with his brother.

Ryan pressed the accelerator, sending throat-clogging dust into the air. In an effort to cut off Russ, who'd climbed from his car and was heading toward the lodge, Ryan slid into a parking spot allowing him to reach Mia first. Truck still rocking from the sudden stop, Ryan hopped out and hurried toward the walkway.

"Thought I told you to stay away from here," Russ said as he reached Ryan.

Ryan shrugged. "This is a free country. I just stopped in to see Mia."

"I could haul you in for interfering in the investigation."

"Try it. I outweigh you." Ryan fixed his gaze on Russ.

Russ clamped his hand on his gun. "Need I say more?"

"Go ahead. Shoot me." Ryan challenged Russ in a tone he might not be able to back down from, but at least Russ would be busy arresting him instead of interrogating Mia.

"Fine… I'll let you stay. But not a word. Even if you think I'm picking on Mia. Got it?"

Ryan nodded, though if Russ got too difficult Ryan fully intended to step in.

Russ took off, climbed the lodge stairs and then pounded on the door. Ryan followed.

Fierce barking sounded from the lodge.

"You think something's wrong?" Ryan asked.

"Don't overreact."

Russ pounded again. Nothing but barking.

He twisted the knob before pushing the door open. "Mia," he called out.

No response. Bandit's barking turned frantic.

Russ withdrew his gun from the holster on his belt. "Stay here."

Stay here?

Not hardly. Ryan had not reacted strongly enough with Cara and she'd ended up dead. He would not make the same mistake with Mia.

Please let us be in time to help Mia.

He followed Russ who'd already moved down the hallway toward the bedrooms. Bandit had stopped barking and was whimpering and scratching at the door of his crate.

"What do you think you're doing?" Mia's voice shot out from the doorway.

Ryan spun around and let out a long breath. "We came to see you but when Bandit started barking and you didn't answer, we thought something might be wrong."

"We?"

"Russ is down the hall." He cupped his hands around his mouth. "Hey, Russ. Mia's out here. She's fine."

Despite his residual concern, he had enough presence of mind to enjoy the sight of a freshly showered Mia. Dressed in a green jogging suit in that soft fuzzy kind of fabric he didn't know the name of, she crossed the room to Bandit and opened his crate.

When she caught sight of the little dog, she smiled like an innocent child. A wide dazzling smile that stole Ryan's breath. She looked downright sensational, and he had to tamp down the urge to greet her with a fierce hug.

"Hey, little fella." She bent over and cupped Bandit's head. He ran his pink tongue over her palm, and she scooped him up. "What's this I hear about you barking?"

Her tone was so gentle and loving, a pang of jealousy coursed through Ryan. It had been three years since a woman had talked to him with such tenderness and he missed the companionship. Maybe he'd been too hasty when he'd sworn off forging a relationship with a woman again. Maybe he could love again and not experience a loss as he had with Cara.

Stowing his gun, Russ clomped into the room. "Good, you're here."

"What can I do for you, Russ?" Mia asked as she walked to the kitchen island and set her purse on to the countertop.

"First off, I wanted to tell you we ID'd the truck in the barn."

"How'd you do that so fast with all the VIN numbers removed?" Ryan joined the pair by the counter.

"Pure luck. The truck belongs to Orrin Jackson. He came back from vacation today and discovered it was stolen."

"Orrin, huh." Ryan said as he processed the news. "He have any ideas who might have taken it?"

"None. But I'm even more convinced this was done by a pro. Orrin's house was ransacked and his gun cabinet emptied."

Mia's face blanched. "So this man is armed, and I may be in real danger?"

"Maybe," Russ said, his tone light and unconcerned like he was dealing with a traffic violation not arson. "More likely the intruder plans to sell the weapons."

"But you can't be sure," Mia said.

"No, I can't be sure." Russ's tone lacked his usual confidence.

Mia turned away but not before Ryan caught a glimpse of her stricken expression.

He lifted a hand to squeeze her shoulder in comfort, but let it fall. She was in more danger than he had earlier believed. Danger like Cara had been in. Danger that would keep him from chasing after those wayward feelings he'd had a few moments ago.

He curled his fingers into a fist and faced Russ. "What do you plan to do about it?"

"There's nothing I can do except get this investigation resolved more quickly." He dug a plastic bag from his pocket and laid it open on his hand. A shiny bracelet settled into his palm.

As Mia stared at the bracelet secured in the bag, Ryan checked it out. He'd never seen this piece of jewelry before, of that he was sure.

"We found this in the box with the hand. I'm certain it's yours." Russ stepped closer to Mia.

She backed up until her feet met a bar stool, and her eyes took on an uncomfortable sheen. She resembled a trapped animal. Ryan held his breath as he waited for her to speak.

"Is this bracelet yours?" Russ shoved his hand closer.

She looked down at the dog still clutched in her arms. Russ moved into her personal space and her head snapped up. At the tightening of her jaw, Ryan's instincts urged him to step in between them, but he wanted to hear the answer as much as Russ did.

"It's not m—"

"Before you deny it," Russ interrupted, "the charms have dates engraved on them. Dates like your birthday." He maneuvered the charms around and jabbed his index finger at a birthday cake.

Shell shocked, she slowly lowered her body on to the stool. Bandit licked her cheek, and she hugged him as if he were a lifeline to sanity.

Ryan didn't need to see or hear anymore. This was Mia's bracelet. Her eyes confirmed her disbelief in seeing it.

So what was her story?

If she had a bracelet that obviously meant a great deal to her, why hadn't she shown it to him all those times she cried over her mother? The only answer that came to mind was one he didn't want to acknowledge. Maybe she hadn't trusted him as much as he'd believed.

Mia released the wiggling Bandit and wrapped her arms around her waist. How could anyone have gotten a hold of her bracelet and put it on that hand? And how did that relate to the threat or the fire?

Maybe this was a setup. Maybe Russ thought he could trick her into confessing to being behind these incidents, but the only thing she could confess was the bracelet was likely hers.

"I had a charm bracelet when I was a kid." Her

voice came out strained when she'd hoped for a lighter tone.

"What happened to it?" Russ asked.

"That's a long story."

"I have time." His tone was sympathetic but she figured he was just using his interrogation skills.

She glanced at Ryan for support she had no right to ask for after the way she'd left things when they last spoke. And she got what she deserved. His eyes were hard and appraising.

Did he think she'd had something to do with the threats? Didn't he know her at all? She wilted under his gaze.

"Mia." Russ held out the bracelet.

She took the bag and spread the thick chain across her open palm. The cool metal slashed a line across her hand. Memories undulated like ocean waves over her back. The bracelet seemed alive, like a snake reaching out to bite her.

She couldn't hold it any longer so she thrust the bag back at Russ. "It's my bracelet, but I don't know how it ended up in that box. It was disposed of the summer I moved here."

"Disposed of?" Russ asked. "How? Where?"

Mia thought about the summer and the loss of her mother. She'd never wanted to speak aloud to anyone about this. She'd certainly never share the gut-wrenching details with Russ. But she could give him enough information to understand that barring a miracle—barring the fact that the evidence was in his hands—this could not be her bracelet.

She'd make the telling brief. She rattled through the details of the car accident then stopped to fight back the tears that always threatened when she thought about that day. She looked at Ryan whose eyes had filled with compassion. Guilt for the way she'd treated him earlier pummeled her heart so she turned to Russ. His sympathetic gaze was nearly her undoing.

If a closed man like Russ empathized with her story, she felt justified in falling apart. It took all the effort she could dredge up to continue. But the sooner she told this, the sooner she could file the memory back in the don't-open-unless-forced file in her brain.

She looked at her feet. "My father was distraught over Mom's death. He didn't want to see anything that reminded him of her, and he certainly didn't want to go back to Atlanta. After deciding we would live here, he convinced Uncle Wally to get rid of everything we owned in Atlanta. Our house and all of our stuff. All Dad let us keep were the things we brought up here. Minus Mom's stuff, of course."

"Sounds harsh," Russ said.

"It was. But hey, we got over it." *Liar. You're still carrying it around like a backpack full of rocks.*

"Wally might not have gotten rid of everything," Ryan said. "Maybe he kept the bracelet."

Mia shook her head. "Not likely. Wally had a

picture of my mom. He gave it to me at her funeral. When my dad found out, he threw it in the fireplace and threatened to kill Wally if he gave me anything else. There's no way anyone would want to stand up to that rage again."

"So if Wally didn't keep it, who does that leave?" Russ asked.

"No one. My dad would never have asked for the bracelet. All of the charms were from special times with Mom. It would bring him too much pain. And David was fifteen. No teenage boy would want his little sister's bracelet."

"Then maybe someone had a replica made," Ryan said more to Russ, than to Mia, as if he felt the need to defend her. "To hurt her. To get her to leave."

She thought about the charms. Could they be duplicated? She ticked them off one at a time, mentally stroking them as she traveled along the length of the silver chain.

When she reached the end, the answer struck her like a bolt of lightning. "Check the penny from Stone Mountain. When you smash a coin in one of those machines, it stamps the year into the copper. They could easily smash the penny, but how would they replicate that date?"

Russ laid the plastic in his palm and flipped the penny over. Mia stared at the bracelet. As it moved, piercing rays shooting through the window glinted from the charms as if the bracelet were sending out a warning.

"1982. This is the real deal." Head bent, Russ jiggled the charms again. "Assuming, and this is a big assumption, this warning and the fire are related, then the bracelet points toward someone from your family. Access to your old bracelet would most likely be restricted to your family and, of course," he looked down on Mia, "you."

As she stared at him in disbelief over his need to keep her on his suspect list, he shoved the bag back into his pocket. "We were able to lift two sets of prints from the charms so that should move us forward."

"Finally, something to go on." She let relief color her words. "And something that will clear my name."

"Not necessarily," he said. "You could have hired someone to put the bracelet in the box just like you did to start the fire."

What? She did not expect him to go in that direction.

Ryan's jaw tightened. "We've been over this, bro. Move on. Mia's not involved in this."

She came to her feet. "He's right, and I can prove it."

"I'm listening," Russ said, cocking a brow.

She reached across the counter and withdrew the first letter along with the will from her purse then thrust them into Russ's hand. "Here's the will. Once you read it, you'll know I don't gain anything until the year is up. In the envelope is a letter that was waiting for me at the post office yesterday."

Russ tucked the will under his arm then opened the envelope and scanned the letter. "Okay, so how does this prove you aren't involved? You could've sent it to yourself."

"Look at the postmark. I was in Atlanta when it was sent."

Russ rolled his eyes. "So the guy you hired to start the fire mailed the letter."

"You're unbelievable," Ryan burst out. "Can't you at least acknowledge you could be wrong and someone is threatening Mia?"

"Despite what you both think about me," Russ paused and looked at them in turn, "I have an open mind. I'm more than willing to entertain another suspect, but so far there doesn't seem to be anyone else good for this."

Ryan advanced on his brother. "How about Mia's father or David for that matter? You could at least look into them."

"And why would I do that?"

Mia held her hand in front of Ryan. "Ryan, don't."

"I'm sorry, Mia, but he needs to hear this." Ryan explained her father and David's motive.

Russ fixed a hard stare on her. "Why is this the first time I'm hearing about this?"

"She hopes to one day reconcile with her father, and she doesn't want people in town to gossip about her like they did back in high school," Ryan answered for her. "That would only make Dr. Black-burn angry."

"I'll talk with your dad and David about this." Russ straightened to full height and tucked the letter into the envelope. "If I have additional questions, I'll get back to you."

"No, wait. Isn't there some way to do this with-out talking to them?" Mia asked, even though she already knew the answer.

"Not if you want me to get to the bottom of this, there isn't." Surprisingly, his tone was sympathetic and his eyes kind before he strode off.

She watched him leave and dug deep to find the confident woman who bolted for cover as she always did when her father was involved.

"You don't look so good," Ryan said.

Her head shot up. "Really?" Her sarcasm hit him like a Mack truck, and she instantly regretted the harsh tone. "I'm sorry. I didn't mean to snap at you, but it hurts to think my father might hate me this much. Not to mention the fact that you've probably started the ball rolling for the news to be spread all over town."

"I'm sorry, Mia, but the stolen guns show how much danger you're in. Even if I don't think your dad is behind this, I had to tell Russ about the letter. It was the only thing I could think of to draw Russ's attention from you." He sighed. "He has to realize someone is threatening you and not waste time trying to prove your guilt."

She knew Ryan spoke the truth, but right now it was a better choice for Russ to blame her than to interrogate her father and David. After Russ questioned them, all hope of reconciling would end and she would be without a family forever.

TEN

Ryan moaned and pushed back his chair. Enough was enough. He'd spent the last two hours in the rec center preparing for the students arrival tomorrow, and he couldn't concentrate with thoughts of the stolen guns and Mia's bracelet weighing heavy on his mind.

The more he thought about the situation, the more certain he felt that her father and David had nothing to do with this. One thing was clear, though. They had no clue who was behind the warnings and with Mia's life in jeopardy he couldn't go on with his normal life. He'd done that with Cara and look how terrible that had turned out.

He had to talk to Mia. Discuss the latest happening and figure out how to bring this to a close.

Outside, he kept his gaze from the counselors working near the fire pit as he didn't want to be distracted from his mission. He traveled to the lodge and knocked on the door. As he heard Bandit's nails clipping across the wooden floor, he stepped back.

A loud thump was followed by laughter and Mia

saying, "You silly dog. You need to be more careful or you'll get brain damage."

She pulled open the door and Bandit charged out. He circled Ryan and danced on his rear feet.

"Ryan," Mia said, a question in her voice.

"Can we talk for a minute? Maybe out here on the porch? I just can't quit thinking about the bracelet and feel like we're missing something." He moved out of her way and gestured toward a chair.

She settled into a rocker.

"My mind keeps coming back to the fact that Wally must have kept the bracelet." He took the chair next to her. "I don't know why, but there's no other possible explanation for how it could have shown up here."

"I'm leaning the same way, but then why didn't he give it to me when I moved to Atlanta? My dad had no hold over either of us then."

Ryan shrugged. "Who knows what he might have been waiting for. But we need to assume he brought it back to Pinetree and someone around here got a hold of it. That's the only way we can move forward. So who might have found it and realized what it was?"

"Only one person has unrestricted access to Wally's stuff up here and that's Verna." Mia's eyes lit up. "She knows all about our family, and she was acting weird when I talked to her this afternoon. You know Wally never locked anything around here so

I asked her why the barn was locked, and she gave me a vague answer then acted all secretive."

"So you think Verna locked the barn to hide something?"

"I don't know. I'm not even sure both doors were locked. I can only vouch for the one I got stuck in."

"There was a chain hanging on the other handle, but I didn't see a lock."

"We can go down there now and check." Mia jumped to her feet.

Ryan held out his hand. "Not so fast, Mia. I know you want to do something, but how does it help us to move forward if we find out it was locked?"

"Because if the padlock is still there and the chain is intact we know the arsonist had to have the key. If he had a key, then maybe that connects him to Verna." She flashed a dazzling smile his way.

Ryan's pulse raced. This was the vibrant Mia he'd once known. This was how he wanted to see her. Happy and free from turmoil.

"C'mon." She danced in place.

"Okay, but we do it my way. Rutting through a burned building is dangerous. You can come with me, but I'll do the looking."

Her happiness deflated a notch. "Fine."

He stood. "Let me get a pair of boots from my truck. And you might want to put Bandit inside or at least leash him so he doesn't get into trouble."

"It'll do him good to go for a walk. I'll get his leash."

She went inside, and Ryan crossed to his truck. He slipped into protective boots and retrieved his pry bar and gloves. He doubted looking at the chain would pan out, but when he saw the exuberance on Mia's face, he'd have offered to pick up every charred hunk of wood in the barn to find a clue.

"Ready?" Mia asked when she joined him.

Before he could answer, Bandit shot off, jerking the leash and pulling Mia along at a fast clip.

"I probably shouldn't have said I'd take Bandit." She laughed as she tried to rein in the frisky pup. "I don't have the first clue on how to take care of a dog."

"How about I give you some pointers when we get done here?"

"That would be great." She looked up at him with the same admiration she'd had for him in high school and a warm feeling spread through his chest.

Did her look mean she might be on the road to trusting in him again? Or had her failure to show up for orientation meant she'd changed her mind about working with him?

With the unsettling news of her bracelet fresh in her mind, he didn't have the heart to bring up the subject earlier. And now with the upbeat mood, he should leave things alone, but he had to know.

"Have you had a chance to look at Eddie's file?"

She shifted the leash to her other hand and faced

him. "I did. In fact I stopped by the rec center for orientation, but you were busy with your staff."

He wanted to shoot his hand into the air and shout yes, but he didn't want to scare her off by his enthusiasm, so he responded with a flat smile.

She grew very still, stopping to assess him with narrowed eyes, and he knew he'd failed to keep his excitement in check.

"You did say we would keep this on a professional level," she said carefully.

He did say that but could he really follow through when she looked at him as she had a few moments ago? Her forgiveness lifted a huge weight, but he also wanted her respect and trust. He raised his face to the tall pines, listening to the chirping birds.

"Ryan? Can we work together?" Her voice had gone soft like she was afraid to hear his response.

He watched a hawk soar through the trees, and he ran a hand through his hair. "You want the easy answer or the truth?" He let his gaze fall on her face again.

"The truth," slipped from her lips like a sigh of the wind rustling the trees.

"I'll do my best to keep my promise, Mia, but I'd be lying if I didn't say that I wanted you to learn to trust me again." He waited for her to bolt, run for cover at his honesty, but she kept her eyes locked on his.

Softness claimed her vibrant green eyes before they drifted closed and long lashes lay on her cheeks.

"I'm not there yet, but I hope at some point I'll be ready to do that."

"Then that's all I can ask for." He sucked in a cleansing breath and shook off the heaviness that had settled over them.

As a counselor, he knew the progress they had already made was amazing, but she needed more time. He glanced at her. A sense of urgency to move forward and restore her faith in him surged through his veins.

Why was this suddenly so important to him? So pressing?

A flash of Cara lying on the floor with a knife lodged in her stomach shot into his brain, chilling him.

Please keep Mia safe, Lord. And if it's Your will, show me the way to earn her respect.

Life could end in a flash and with the warnings growing more threatening, he might not have all the time in the world to gain Mia's respect and trust.

Mia watched Ryan's body tense up so as they walked she engaged him in conversation about Wilderness Ways to lighten the mood. It didn't take him long to relax and settle into a comfortable banter with her. She enjoyed walking next to him much the same way they had as teens. Liked it more than she cared to admit. There was a warm current of some sort floating around them and it reminded her of when they were so well-connected they could finish each other's sentences.

She glanced up at his face that conveyed he was as contented as she was. But she couldn't let that feeling lead her into making another mistake with him. As much as he wanted her to trust him, she couldn't. Maybe never would. She needed to focus on finding out who was threatening her, not on something that was likely never to come about.

Bandit tugged on his leash, and she changed her focus to the barn. Her mood soured. The north wall where she'd been trapped remained standing, but the rest of the barn huddled on the ground in mounds of ashes and charred wood. The closer they came, the stronger the noxious scent grew. The water-laden ground sucked at her shoes. She picked up Bandit to keep his injured leg clean and moved on. Each step took concentration so she wouldn't slip into the slimy muck.

Sadly, this was exactly the way she'd felt since Uncle Wally died. Like all her positive energy had been sucked from her, and she had to fight with each step from going under. But no more. She'd keep moving forward—no matter the challenge.

Ryan suddenly spun around. "This is as far as you go."

Feeling belligerent from the loss of control in her life, Mia wanted to argue, but he was giving of his time to help her so she acquiesced and nodded her understanding.

He slipped on gloves and picked his way through the debris. His steps were slow and measured until he reached the spot where the main entrance would have been. "The door is still partially standing," he yelled as he bent to dig through the charred wood.

She tried to be patient but as time passed, she had to see if he'd found anything. Careful not to get her shoes too mucky, she tiptoed closer. "What's going on?"

He stood. "There's no chain."

"What? There has to be a chain. You said you saw it the day of the fire."

He stepped through the debris to join her. "Well, there's nothing there now. Maybe Russ took it for evidence."

"Not likely Russ even knew the lock had any significance."

"Only one way to be sure." Ryan pulled off his gloves and stuffed them in his back pocket then reached for his cell.

"Are you sure you want to ask him? It might make him come back here again."

"I can ask in a way that he won't suspect a thing." Ryan dialed, but Mia's mind went to the puzzle and tuned him out.

Assuming Russ didn't take the chain, why would it be gone? Did someone come get it to hide the fact that the barn was locked?

Mia listened as Ryan smooth-talked his brother before saying goodbye.

"He didn't take it." He tucked the phone in his pocket.

"This is really odd," Mia said, letting her gaze rove over the barn. "We should go check the other door to see if that chain is gone, too."

Ryan's eyes narrowed. "No. It's too dangerous. Even for me. That wall could fall over with a slight breeze, and I won't risk getting trapped under the debris."

"But I have to know."

His eyes met hers. "Not today, you don't."

"There has to be a way." Disappointed, Mia looked away.

"I'll call the chief and see if he can get the crew together to safely bring the wall down. Then, and only then, will we check on the lock."

She didn't like his answer, but she respected his professional opinion.

"Mia." He gently clasped her shoulders and angled her to face him. "I mean it. Keep away from the barn."

She'd listen to him. For now. But if he didn't arrange to have the wall brought down tomorrow, she'd check it out. Regardless of his warning to take care, she had to see if the lock was still there. Her life could be in peril near an unstable wall, but she'd rather take the risk than sit around and wait for the creep behind the letters to strike again.

ELEVEN

The next morning, as Mia finalized her preparations to head to David's office, she heard a car pull up and park in front of the lodge. She opened the blinds and spotted a hot-pink Cadillac. A large woman wearing a boisterous floral housedress with lime green terrycloth slippers climbed from the driver's side.

Mia groaned. Where could she hide?

Mrs. Miller, the town busybody who should be classified as one of the Eight Wonders of the World, flapped her hands in the air as she jabbered at the scrawny Mr. Miller wearing faded bib overalls exiting the passenger side of the car.

Despite the woman's reputation, her wild gestures and animated face piqued Mia's interest. With all of Mrs. Miller's contacts, she may have heard gossip about the incidents and could lead them to a clue.

Mia left the lodge and met the pair at the end of the sidewalk where Mrs. Miller charged as if she'd just spotted a two-for-one sale on muumuus. "Here you are, Mia, you poor dear."

"Hello, Mrs. Mil—"

She waved a plump hand. "Oh, no, no, no. You're all grown-up now. Call us Frank and Gladys."

"If that's what you want." Mia watched the pink foam curler perched at the crown of Gladys's head bob up and down.

Gladys stepped closer. "I won't take up much of your time when you should be resting from that dreadful fire, but I have something that might help find the arsonist."

Just as Mia had hoped. "What is it, Mrs. Mil—Gladys?"

Her eyes turned conspiratorial. "I was at Reid's place last night checking on little Jessie. Russ showed up and while I played cards with the little sweetie, he and Reid went into the other room. They thought they were out of earshot, but I heard them talking about the man Jessie saw start the fire." She paused with a beam of satisfaction lighting her face.

Mia didn't think Gladys was playing cards. Knowing her, she had her ear snugged up to the door to learn all she could.

"I also heard the truck belonged to Orrin Jackson. Probably stolen by the man who started the fire. Now who would go stealing Orrin's truck like that? Not anyone from around here, I tell you. Jessie confirmed that. She can't identify that man as a local, but then at her age, she doesn't know everyone in town."

"So what do you propose?" Mia asked.

"I'm just getting to that. A couple years ago, the hubby and I," she paused to give Frank a pointed look, "got tired of city slickers passing bad checks and bogus credit cards at the station. So we started scanning a copy of strangers' licenses and credit cards when they made a purchase. So, if the man who stole the truck and started the fire bought gas with a credit card, I'd have a copy of his license."

Mia managed not to laugh at the outrageous idea. "This guy wouldn't be too smart to bring a stolen truck into your station."

"Oh, I know that, but if he's not from around here, he had to get to Logan Lake to steal the truck. Maybe whatever he was driving needed gas. Or he got hungry and needed a snack." She dug in her bag and withdrew a red case. "Last night I went through all of the files for the last few months and pulled out the pictures of men matching Jessie's description. They're all right here on this DVD." She slipped the case into Mia's hand.

"Sounds like a long shot, but maybe it'll pay off." Mia smiled her thanks. "I'll look at it when I get a chance."

"That's good. Be sure to tell me if I can help with anything else." She paused and studied Mia. "I just can't believe you're back and you'll be our neighbor for the next year. I know your father and David are so happy you've come home." She winked. "Why at church last Sunday they were jabbering on about how good it will be to have the family reunited."

Mia wished what Gladys said was truth, but her

father had often gone to church with his game face on, making believe their family was coping well.

Gladys slipped her hand through the crook of Mia's arm. "I dare say Ryan's glad to have you back, too."

Mia did not want to go there with Gladys but Mia recalled that trying to ignore this woman always ended up spurring her on. "I suppose he's grateful to have me fill in for his missing counselor."

Gladys swatted her hand at Mia. "That's not what I mean. I don't know if you heard about the terrible tragedy Ryan faced in Eugene."

Mia didn't want to egg Gladys on, but this must be why Ryan had clammed up in the truck and Mia wanted to know more. "I hadn't heard about that."

"It was terrible. Just terrible. He was engaged to a sweet little woman. Another counselor he worked with. One of her clients killed her. Stabbed her in the very office they worked in. Ryan, the poor man, found her alive, but there was nothing he could do." Gladys tugged her closer. "Rumor has it he feels responsible. Like he should have been able to protect her."

Mia couldn't speak. She knew his pain. For she'd experienced the same heartbreak when her mother had died.

"I know how much you cared about him at one time," Gladys said, her tone sincere. "He's basically sworn off women, and I think you're just the person to change that. If you got together w—"

"Let it be, Gladys. You've meddled enough for the day." Frank stepped between them and pried away Gladys's hand. He held Gladys by the shoulder.

"Let me go, Frank Miller." Gladys ripped free and waddled to the car. She spun on Frank. "Well, what are you waiting for, Frank, an engraved invitation? Let's go."

Mia's mind filled with this unsettling news. She watched the odd couple climb into their car and drive off.

Poor Ryan. From what he'd said yesterday, it had only been three years since his fiancée's death. A death that left him feeling responsible.

Guilt over such a thing was powerful. Life altering. Changing one's approach on life. This explained his overreaction to the warnings. He was afraid the same thing was going to happen to her. Afraid the creep who sent the warning letters might carry out his threats.

A chill seeped into her bones. If she didn't figure out who was behind the warning, Ryan could turn out to be right.

Residual unease from Gladys's news and uncertainty over seeing David after such a long absence left Mia a basket case as she opened the door to his office. She greeted his secretary, Olivia, but didn't like how fragile her voice sounded.

The sweet young woman's widening smile said she hadn't noticed. "David's been looking forward to seeing you ever since he heard you were coming home." She settled back into her chair, her size dwarfed by the tall leather back. "You can go on back. He's in Kurt's office, the last one on the right."

If he was looking forward to seeing her, why was he with his partner? Was David as uneasy about their meeting again after a ten-year absence? "I'm not interrupting anything, am I?"

Olivia waved a hand with fingernails painted in a plum color that matched her silk blouse. "Not at all. Kurt handles Pinetree's accounts so David figured you'd want to meet him while you were here."

Hoping Olivia was right and David really was happy she'd come to visit, Mia set off down the hallway. The hope didn't travel to her feet as they slowed when she reached the office with Kurt Loomis, CPA engraved on the door. She let her eyes sweep the room.

A man Mia assumed was Kurt sat behind the desk covered in paperwork that looked as if it had settled after a tornado. A large ornate frame holding the picture-perfect family of two girls and a boy, accompanied by a smiling couple hung on the wall behind him.

David, his back to her, sat beside the massive antique desk. The men engaged in an animated discussion about returns on investment, their tones speaking to the love of a job Mia couldn't imagine choosing. Much like she couldn't imagine actually talking to her brother after all these years. But that was why she was here.

She knocked on the door and waited for an invitation to enter.

Kurt came to his feet, a wide smile pulling up full lips. A white dress shirt snugged tight at his neck with a navy tie accenting his fair coloring. He had a kind face that welcomed her into the room.

David rose and pivoted. He wore a power business suit with a striped tie. He held his shoulders back in a rigid stance as his appraising eyes took in her entrance.

Painful memories captured her mind. Not of David, but her father. David was a photocopy of their father when he was younger. His expression, his eyes, his lips. The entire package said Dad.

She took a step back and thought about bolting.

His face mirrored her discomfort as he adjusted his tie in a nervous gesture. He approached and lifted his arms as if he might try to hug her.

She wasn't ready for that, so she thrust her hand out instead. "Good to see you, David."

His charcoal eyes darkened, but he didn't lose a beat and shook her hand. She gave him a minimal shake, withdrew her hand and pushed the strap of her handbag higher on her shoulder to mask her sudden action.

David's eyes telegraphed his confusion but he recovered quickly. He gestured at Kurt. "This is my partner, Kurt Loomis. He handles Pinetree's accounts, so I asked him to join us."

"Then I'm happy to meet you, Kurt," Mia said with honest enthusiasm and held out her hand. "I don't know the first thing about running a business. I have to count on Verna to do the bookkeeping and you to do whatever it is you do."

"Actually, Verna doesn't really do the bookkeeping anymore." Kurt clasped her fingers with a warm shake, his face earnest, and his gray eyes sincerely welcoming. "When we took over the accounts a few years back, we set up a system to be more GAAP friendly."

Mia's mind went blank, and she looked at David for help.

He chuckled. "Excuse Kurt's lack of English. GAAP is an acronym for generally accepted accounting principals. In this case, we separated the duties of taking in the money from spending the money. So Verna takes it in, and Kurt pays the bills. Keeps everyone on the up and up." David clasped his hands behind his back. "So what is it you wanted to see us about?"

"Ah…no…I didn't come to talk about the business. This is more of a personal call."

"Oh." David's surprise flashed across his face.

Mia instantly regretted coming. Why did she think he wanted to have anything to do with her? Her brother had always sided with their father in the past. He was likely still under his influence.

She'd give him an out. "If you don't have time, I can go…"

"No. No. That's fine. Let's go to my office."

"Nice to meet you, Mia," Kurt said. "I'm preparing financial reports for you and once they're finished we can get together to review them."

Mia's forehead crinkled in distaste.

Kurt laughed. "I promise to help you understand them."

"Thanks, Kurt. It was nice meeting you, too," Mia replied with a smile. She really liked David's partner. Maybe once she and David broke the ice, he'd warm up the same way.

He led her down the hall to an office similar to Kurt's in size, but casual in design. He'd decorated in muted beiges with blue accents reflecting the personality she'd seen in the last few minutes. With a slight nod, he urged Mia to sit on a thick leather sofa.

She complied while looking at the multitude of family pictures perched around the room. On the table next to her sat a candid shot of their father with two adorable girls grinning into his face as he returned the smile with such love flowing from his eyes that Mia almost ceased breathing.

"That's Dad and my girls after Easter services," David said. "Maybe now that you're in town you can come over and meet Peg and the girls."

Mia recovered from the shock of seeing the picture of their father enough to respond with a pleasant, "That would be nice."

David casually sat back, crossing his legs and acting as if she'd simply taken a little time away rather than ten years. Like a long vacation.

Had he forgotten about their tumultuous past? Why she left? If so, he wouldn't think their father had any part in these events.

He shifted as if growing uncomfortable under her scrutiny. "So what did you want to talk about?"

She reached into her purse and pulled out her copy of the threatening letter. "You said you'd heard about the fire, but there's something else I need to tell you about. I was wondering if you could look at this. It's a copy of a letter I received in the mail. The envelope had a Logan Lake postmark. Do you have any idea who might've sent it to me?"

David opened the letter and sat forward. "Do you think this person set fire to the barn?"

She nodded. "Any idea of who'd want me to leave town this badly?"

David ran a hand through thick hair gleaming with some sort of product and leaving behind little tufts standing at attention. "I guess if you're looking for someone who would profit from your leaving, it would be me." A sincere smile curled his lips. "But I really meant it when I said you deserve Pinetree. So I hope you don't think I'd do something like this."

Mia wanted to return the smile but he looked so much like their father she couldn't bring herself to follow through. But it did help her gather the courage to continue. "I was kind of wondering if Dad might've done this."

His back straightened. "Dad? No way! How could you even think that?"

"He's never made it a secret of the fact that I embarrass him. Seems like he'd be happy if I didn't stay around here and sully his reputation more."

"That's crazy."

"Wait, there's more," Mia said. "This morning I received a package with a second warning. The box contained a fake severed hand, and my old charm bracelet. I haven't seen that bracelet since before Mom died and suddenly it appears on the wrist of a severed hand."

David's face drained of color. "So where did it come from?"

"That's the thing...I don't know. Wally was supposed to get rid of the bracelet when he cleaned out our house in Atlanta, but he must have kept it. Then someone got a hold of it. Someone who knew how much it meant to me and used it to scare me."

"And you think Dad did this?"

"I don't want to, but who else knew how much the memories would hurt me?"

David sat in silence, his eyes distant.

"Think about it, David. Dad is the logical choice."

"Not to me he's not," David said, his voice vehement. "Look, Mia, I know the two of you didn't get along, but after my girls were born, he talked to me about the mistakes he made with you and told me how sorry he is about it."

"Then why didn't he try to contact me?"

"He didn't think you'd take his call."

"That's a lame excuse." Anger coursed through her over the thought of so many wasted years, and she shot to her feet. "I refuse to believe he wanted to make up with me and then didn't even try. I have to proceed by thinking he's behind it."

David frowned and let his eyes linger on hers. "You do what you have to do, Mia, but please don't tell Dad you think he did this." He rose and handed her the letter. "He's already hesitant when it comes to reconciling with you, and he may never try if you accuse him of something this horrible."

Mia slipped the letter back into her purse and said goodbye. She'd be more than happy to entertain David's advice, but after her conversation with their father at the hospital, the irreversible damage had already been done.

TWELVE

Nearing the end of the Wilderness Ways orientation with Mia, Ryan leaned over her shoulder. The sweet aroma of her perfume drifted upward as if inviting him to move closer as it had for the last few hours. Or was it the memory of her stricken expression after speaking with David that enticed him to hold her close?

Didn't matter. He couldn't succumb. Not as long as her life was in danger. Maybe never.

He needed to remove the temptation and put some space between them.

He moved to the other end of the table and then perched on the corner. "That last form is a release for the documentary."

"What documentary?" She glanced up at him then back at the paper.

"I thought I'd told you about that."

"No." She sat back and peered up at him.

"With increased cuts in funding, I need to find new revenue sources to keep the program running. I hired a documentary crew to film this session so

I can use it in fundraising. Not the private counseling times, but group and wilderness activities." He shrugged. "You probably won't end up on tape, but we need your permission just in case."

"Fine by me." She turned back to the form and trailed a finger down the page as she read.

He studied the top of her head. He'd loved her riotous red hair in high school and wished she hadn't changed it. The natural color reminded him that a temper matching the fiery color lurked inside of her and she was known to let it fly at times. Much the same way she had with him since she'd arrived. More than that, though, the memory of how easy it was to slide his fingers into the tangles and draw her close for a kiss pounded his brain.

He lurched to his feet and went to the other side of the table. This line of thinking was unacceptable. He needed something solid between them. Not that Mia noticed him at all. She scribbled her name on a form then turned to the next set of documents.

Her cell lying on the table vibrated, drawing her head up.

"David," she said. "Mind if I take this?"

"Go ahead." Ryan went to the window to find something to look at other than her. He listened to her side of the conversation. Apparently, David was inviting her to dinner tonight and she was trying to wiggle out of it.

Ryan opened the blinds and peered over the lake. Sharp explosive cracks shot through the air in the distance. Probably teens playing with firecrackers. These fireworks were illegal in Oregon, but that didn't stop people from firing them off any more than his determination not to get involved with Mia had tamped down the fireworks between them.

As her resigned tone caught his attention, he turned to look at her.

She massaged her forehead and sighed. "Let me check with Ryan."

"David wants me to meet him for dinner at six. Will we be done in time?"

Ryan nodded.

"I can come," she said into the phone followed by another sigh. She listened for a few moments, her eyes closing like clenched fists then reopening before she handed the cell to Ryan. "He wants to talk to you."

Eyes searching hers for a clue as to what David might want, Ryan took the phone. "David."

"With all the crazy things happening around there, I'm concerned about Mia being out at night by herself. Would you be willing to come to dinner with her?"

Ryan suppressed a groan. With the sudden wave of emotions still fresh in his mind, he didn't need to be in her company for more time than absolutely necessary. "I'm not sure that's such a good idea."

"I'd come pick her up myself, but I have a late appointment. Who knows what could happen if she was out at night alone."

David was right. Ryan couldn't let Mia go off on her own tonight. He'd let Cara do that and she died. He wouldn't risk Mia's life, too.

Gaze locked with Ryan's, Mia took the phone from him. Raw emotions flashed in his eyes, and his breathing had deepened. She wanted to question David about what had transpired during their brief conversation, but wouldn't do so with Ryan standing nearby.

She finished her conversation with David and returned her phone to the table. "So you're going to dinner tonight, too?"

His head bobbed in a clipped nod then he looked at the clock. "Time for your session. I'll get Eddie for you." Ryan met her eyes with a lingering stare then took off for the door.

What was with that last look? Was he upset because he didn't want to go to David's tonight? Or did seeing her in danger remind him of Cara?

His guilt and pain over Cara might be behind his fluctuating behavior, but Mia couldn't change that, even if she understood his motives. She should tell him to forget dinner tonight, but selfishly she was hoping he'd help break the ice with David.

She clenched and relaxed her hands to ease out tension. This relationship was far too complicated and too personal. They promised to work together as professionals, but after a few hours on the job, that possibility was waning fast.

But she couldn't let down Eddie and the other students. She'd simply have to make sure she and Ryan kept things strictly businesslike. Her mind reeling, she decided to stretch her legs and get some fresh air so she wasn't tense and closed down for Eddie.

She left the office and entered the main room of the rec center. She searched the room for Ryan and Eddie. Instead, she spotted her father and a nurse talking near medical screens set up in the corner. Her steps faltered as she studied him. Ryan told her a doctor performed a brief physical on the students to confirm their ability to handle the extreme conditions, but he hadn't said the doctor would be her father.

Rattled, she resumed her steps, picking up speed. Her athletic shoes squeaked as she walked and a group of students mimicked the sound drawing attention to the noise. She glanced at her father. He'd spotted her. She assumed he'd ignore her, but he patted the nurses shoulder then set out in Mia's direction. They met near the exit blocked by students and counselors filing out of the room.

"Mia," her father said. "I heard you were working with the students." He spoke as if they were friends, leaving her confused.

"I hadn't heard the same about you."

"Dr. Rucker had an emergency so I'm filling in until he can get here." He twisted a rubber band between his fingers. "This is a good thing you're doing here, Mia. Helping these kids. I'm real proud of you."

Proud of her? Who was he to be proud of her after he'd ignored her for so many years? She didn't know how to respond other than to gape at him.

He tipped his head at the corner. "Looks like I have a student waiting on me. Keep up the good work, Mia."

Unsettled, she watched him cross the room. Was it possible he really did want to reconcile with her as David said? Or more likely, had he been behind all the events around here and he was trying to cover his tracks?

The room closed in on her and she needed air. She squeezed through the remaining students at the door and crossed the lawn. Sydney, pacing and checking her watch rushed forward. She grabbed Mia's arm then dragged her behind a stand of junipers.

"What's up?" Mia's alarm rose as she studied Sydney's tightened face.

"I just heard you'd be working with these kids." Sydney's voice had a panicked edge to it. "My little sister, Nikki, hopes to major in filmmaking after high school. She'll be shadowing the documentary staff for the next few days."

Why would this bother Sydney? "That'll be a good experience for her."

Sydney waved a hand. "Oh, I know that, but Nikki's kind of flighty, and I'm worried about her hanging around the kids in the program. Do you think you could keep an eye out for her and tell me if she's getting into any trouble?"

Mia smiled over Sydney's concern for a little sister who sounded far tamer than Sydney ever was in high school. "I'll be happy to do that."

Sydney pointed toward the driveway. "That's her. On the sidewalk by the big guy with the camera."

Mia studied the pixie face with auburn hair and three pounds of eye makeup. Nikki was cute in a high school kind of way, but Sydney, wearing a navy sweater and jeans, was stunning.

Nikki looked up, and Sydney pulled Mia deeper into the trees. "I don't want her to see me."

Mia gave a solemn nod she thought Sydney's sisterly concern deserved.

"I also thought you might like to know that Verna hasn't contacted the insurance company yet. You want me to call you when she does?"

Mia appreciated Sydney looking out for her interests, but she hated to have Sydney spy for her. "Thanks, but I'll follow up with Verna."

"Okay." Sydney peeked around the trees. "Gotta go before Nikki sees me. Catch you later. And thanks." She skittered away, staying under the cover of trees lining the driveway.

Mia was thankful for Sydney's drama. It took her mind off her father's revelation long enough to regain enough composure to go back to the students. She eased out of the trees and rounded the corner while keeping an eye on the parade of students.

Pain radiated from some faces, anger and frustration from others. Ryan stood at the end of the sidewalk deep in a discussion with a counselor. He listened with a keen interest and concerned face. He had such a heart for these students and the counselors who worked for him. She was beginning to see what a good man he'd turned out to be.

He looked her way and offered a quick smile before turning back to his conversation. A conciliatory smile. All business as he'd promised. As she wanted.

Then why did warmth flow through her as she studied him? He'd dressed much the same as yesterday—dark jeans frayed at the bottom, hiking boots, a deep brown suede jacket open and revealing a bright orange T-shirt, all giving him a rustic male charm that was far too attractive.

He clapped his hand on the counselor's back and turned to face her. Their eyes met.

Caught watching him, her first instinct was to pull away, but his lips curled in a soft little smile bringing one to her lips and instantly chipping at her resolve to keep things professional.

Unaware of her discomfort, he joined her and tipped his head at a scowling student. "There's Eddie. I'll get him."

Mia took in the teen with blond hair pulled back in a short ponytail and wearing oversize clothes. His untied Adidas sloshed on his feet, and his shoulders sagged as Ryan escorted the teen closer.

His fierce glare gave her a moment of unease.

Not like Ryan's earlier behavior had. Thankfully, he'd put aside whatever had been on his mind and wore his professional hat as he introduced Eddie. So as she led Eddie into the building, why did she feel let down? Did she want this attraction to Ryan to go somewhere after all?

From his position near the fire pit, Ryan saw Eddie storm down the hill from the rec center. His posture and face clearly communicated anger. Could be a good sign or bad. Depending on his reason for the anger.

Ryan approached Eddie. "Session go okay?"

He scowled. "Was lame. She wanted me to talk about my feelings."

"Good. That's what you need to do. Get your feelings out so you can move forward."

"Ohh, feelings," Eddie said, his sarcasm dripping on each word.

"Listen, Eddie. You have to cooperate if you want to stay in this program. And that means taking the counseling sessions seriously. Go ahead and join the group, but spend some time thinking about this and decide if you really want to be here."

Eddie stomped off, his sloppy Adidas sending up dirt puffs. Ryan directed his gaze toward the rec center. He'd expected Mia to accompany Eddie, but she was nowhere in sight. An uneasy feeling landed in his gut. Had something happened to her or had she merely needed time to write up her counseling session with Eddie?

The students were all actively engaged with the staff so he'd excuse himself and go check on her.

Heading for the rec center, Ryan's unease grew, and he broke into a jog. His cell rang and he pulled it from his belt.

"What's up, Russ?" he asked through uneven breaths.

"Do you know where Mia is?" His tone was cautious.

"Why?"

"We had a report of gunshots in the area. I checked it out. Someone shot up the lodge and left another warning note for Mia."

"I'll be right there," Ryan said while upping his speed.

Please let this end, Lord.

He was such an idiot. Thinking the explosions he'd heard were firecrackers when someone was shooting at the lodge. At least Mia had been with him at the time so he knew she hadn't been hurt.

Unless of course, she headed back to the lodge after her session with Eddie and the gunman lay in wait for her.

THIRTEEN

In the back classroom of the rec center, Mia stared at the computer monitor. She should be typing away, documenting Eddie's visit, but she couldn't concentrate. Not that Eddie's session was boring. Quite the opposite. He'd slouched in the chair across from her, a sullen expression firmly lodged on his face, his tattooed arms tightly crossed. Occasionally he'd offered a sarcastic response to her probing questions, but said nothing to give her insight into his feelings.

She could certainly identify with his actions. She'd behaved the same way after her mother died and her father retreated into his own world. So why couldn't she focus on finding a way to help the teen? He certainly needed help or he was headed down a one-way street of self-destruction. And she desperately wanted to help him, so why was her mind wandering?

She got up and bent over to touch her toes, stretching stiff muscles that she'd strained in rescuing Jessie from the fire. The fire. That was something she could focus on. Especially the terrifying minutes that had ticked by when she was trapped in the blazing barn with her thoughts consumed by her imminent death. Thoughts that continued to hover near the surface, begging to take over.

Straightening up, she twisted her torso and swung her arms to the side. She'd been lucky. She had stiff muscles and a few gashes on her abdomen, but she was alive. Alive and embracing all of her old habits just like Ryan had said. She wanted to control everyone and everything around her.

So what? It had served her well. It was the only way she'd endured all the pain and turmoil life continued to throw at her. Sure, after surviving a tragedy many people experienced a rebirth or change in priorities, and she hadn't, but that didn't mean anything. Right?

Maybe she didn't feel like a survivor yet and wouldn't until the lunatic terrifying her was caught and put in jail. *If* he was caught.

No. She would not think that way. She would think positively. Russ would find a clue and arrest the creep before he tried something else. Yes, that's what he'd do. She needn't let those reoccurring thoughts interfere with her work any longer.

She returned to the table and set to work on Eddie's report. Her fingers flew over the keyboard until she heard Ryan shouting her name from the main room. His tone was saturated with worry, stopping her fingers midair. Her pulse kicked up speed and she hurried to the large room to find out what had him so upset.

Face pale, he raced across the room. "Thank goodness you're all right."

"Why wouldn't I be all right?"

He pulled her close and clamped his strong arms around her like a vise.

A shuddering breath that shook his back, ratcheted up her concern. "You're scaring me, Ryan. What's going on?"

He leaned back, but kept her in the circle of his arms. "Russ just called me. Someone fired gunshots at the lodge and left another warning tacked on the door."

"Gunshots?" Her heart raced. "Was anyone hurt?"

"No. Thank goodness."

She sighed out a breath of relief and extricated herself from his arms. "Did Russ mention what the warning letter said?"

"No, and I didn't ask. I wanted to get up here as fast as I could to make sure you were still here."

She appreciated his concern but the intense emotion blazing from his eyes left her uncomfortable. "I suppose I need to go over there. I'll have to finish my report later."

"Don't worry about the report." He slipped his hand around her elbow. "My truck is outside. I'll drive you."

Mia didn't like the way he was usurping her control and taking charge again. After what had happened to his fiancée, he seemed driven to prevent another horrific ending with Mia, but that didn't change how she felt. She was a grown woman and didn't need a man to take care of her. Especially not one she hadn't yet found a reason to trust.

On the porch, Ryan stared at the door holding a large red target with Mia's picture in the middle. Starting at the outer circle, bullets had pierced each ring leading up to her photo. A message said, *Leave town or my next bullet is for you.*

Not a single shot had missed the target. Whoever was trying to scare Mia had the ability to end her life in a split second if he chose. Ryan was good and worried, but she seemed to take the warning in stride. She sat in a rocker, cradling a frightened Bandit in her arms and cooing softly to calm him down. Ryan wanted to shake her and make her face up to the danger surrounding her, but he didn't have the heart to hurt her more.

Maybe Russ, who finished giving instructions to his deputies and headed their way, would be able to break through that thick shell of hers.

"The little fella doing okay?" Russ tipped his head at Bandit.

"He's still shaking."

Ryan was all for making sure Bandit was okay, but Russ needed to cut to the chase and tell them what he'd learned.

"Any leads?" Ryan asked.

"All we know at this point is that the recovered slugs are .30-06."

"Could they be from one of the guns taken when the truck was stolen?" Mia asked.

"Won't know unless we locate the gun, but I wouldn't count on it. .30-06 is a common caliber for a hunting rifle. Don't have to tell you how many hunters we have around here."

"So, what happens next?" Ryan asked.

"We'll finish processing the scene, which includes figuring out where the shooter was positioned. Maybe we'll catch a break and find a lead there." He peered at Mia. "Have you thought of anything else I need to know since we last spoke?"

"No."

"Did you talk to her father and David?" Ryan inquired.

"I did, but I have to say I don't like either one of them for this."

"And what are you basing that on?" Mia's tone was wary.

"Just my gut instinct. I'm a pretty good judge of people and they both seemed sincerely glad you'd come home."

"But your gut says I'm guilty?" Mia's sarcasm hit the mark as if she'd slapped his face.

He ran a hand around the neck of his shirt and tugged on the collar. "Actually, no. I reviewed the will with our attorneys." His gaze softened. "It's clear you don't stand to gain anything before your year is up. I can see no motive for you to be involved in this. I apologize for accusing you."

"Apologize? You?" Ryan's tone skittered high as he raised his brows.

"When I'm wrong, I say I'm wrong."

Ryan snorted. "Not hardly."

"Well, in this case, I am." Russ turned sincere eyes to Mia. "Hope you'll accept my apology."

Her eyes softened and she nodded.

Ryan let his gaze linger on Mia. She seemed relieved. He should feel relief also, but if Russ was right and neither her father nor David were involved in the incidents, that left some crazy stranger as the prime suspect. Someone who was an expert shooter and was out to get Mia.

Mia breathed in deeply and let air whoosh out as she set Bandit on the ground. Letting him run off his fear should relax him, but how was she supposed to calm down after seeing the target filled with bullet holes? A mere hour had passed since she'd convinced herself that this terror would end soon. Now she was faced with another threat. This one was not a vague warning, but a direct threat to her life.

How did she go on from here? Could she act like nothing had happened and resume her life? She'd put up a good front for Ryan and Russ but her inner turmoil was reaching the eruption point. If she had any hope of moving forward she needed to use this walk with Bandit to gain control of and reorder her thoughts.

She traipsed behind him, and Ryan caught up to her. "How are you holding up?"

"Honestly? Not so good. I just want Russ to figure out who's doing this and make it stop."

"At least he's ruled you out as a suspect."

She smiled tightly. "Do you think he's right about my father?"

"As much as it appears he's the most likely suspect, yeah, I think Russ is right. Your father may have hurt you in high school, Mia, but I don't think it was intentional. He just didn't know how to recover from his grief. But this," he waved a hand at the barn as they approached the ruins, "this was done on purpose."

One part of her felt relief that her father hadn't intentionally hurt her, giving hope for reconciliation. The other part of her was terrified to find out who willingly would do something as harsh as blast bullets into the lodge and burn down the barn.

Bandit shot off, racing toward the end of the barn with the standing wall.

"No, boy, come back," she called out, going after him and climbing under the yellow crime-scene tape.

Bandit kept running until he reached the far corner of the barn and sniffed around in the rubble. He yipped in little excited barks.

"Hold up, Mia." Ryan stopped her forward progress

with a tug of the arm. "There's no way I'll let you go any closer. I'll get him."

She'd had just about enough of Ryan telling her what to do, but she wouldn't argue now when Bandit could be in danger. With Ryan's training he was the logical person to retrieve the wayward dog.

Ryan called out in a soothing voice that did little to calm Bandit. Hands clenched in fists, she stood like a dolt feeling useless. She looked around. The door she'd been trapped in was only ten feet away. As long as she was standing there, she should take a quick peek at the lock.

She glanced at Ryan to be sure he was still heading toward Bandit before she took careful steps through the thick muck to the door. The handles remained intact. But no chain. No lock. Just like the other end. The lock could only have been removed with a key or cutters. She squatted and picked at the rubble to look for other clues. Nothing but charred wood and muck.

Pushing to her haunches, she grabbed the door handle to keep her shifting feet steady. The wood gave way. The rush of the door, combined with soggy soil sucked her forward. She groped around, hoping for anything to keep from falling. The wall collapsed under her weight.

The charred lumber exploded in an ash-laden cloud and a loud crash of timber.

She landed with a plop, gray particles settling

around her body. She inhaled and coughed out the chest-clogging dust.

Oh, no. Ryan and Bandit.

Had her foolishness hurt them? She had to find them.

She pushed to her feet.

"Are you okay?" Ryan yelled from the other end of the barn.

She looked up. He stood, safe and unharmed. Thank goodness.

"Where's Bandit?" she screamed and plodded through the murky gunk toward him.

Ryan bent down and lifted the dirty dog into his arms. As he rose to his full height, he paused and released a shudder. He shook his head then peered at her with eyes creased in heart-wrenching pain.

Mia arrived next to him and scanned his body for injury. "Are you hurt?"

"No, I'm fine."

"Then why the face?"

"It's nothing. Let's go up to the lodge and get cleaned up." He stepped in front of her and tried to turn her around.

"What's wrong? Are you mad at me for checking on the lock?"

"No. Now come on." He grabbed her arm and let eyes dark with emotion connect with hers.

Fear rising up her back, she shook off his hand. Something major was wrong. He didn't chastise her for causing the wall collapse. And his eyes held something she'd never seen in the brilliant blue before. Fear. Raw and primal.

"What are you not telling me, Ryan? Is there something in there?"

"Nothing you need to see."

Who was he to protect her all the time? She was a capable woman. She could handle whatever he'd discovered. After all, it couldn't be as bad as seeing the lodge all shot up.

She forced her way past him, letting her eyes rove over the area.

She gasped. Sucked in a cleansing breath but pulled in a stench so foul it brought tears to her eyes. "Oh, no. No. No."

Why had she been so stubborn? Hadn't she learned anything yesterday?

Panicked, she turned to run.

Ryan snagged her hand and drew her into the protective shield of his arms alongside Bandit. She not only let Ryan hold her, she clung to him, and laid her head on his solid chest that thumped at a rate matching her accelerated speed.

He was right again.

She didn't need to see that body trapped under a charred stack of wood.

FOURTEEN

On the lodge's porch, Ryan stroked Bandit's soft hair and kept his eyes on Russ. He snapped picture after picture of the body while Ryan's mind fixed on the discovery as if it had taken pictures he'd never be able to erase.

Two legs, calf down, jutted from intact bales lying perpendicular to the body. Wood resembling dropped pixie sticks lay on top. Khaki trousers and expensive leather loafers were the only visible clues to the corpse's identity. The fire had not reached the body so identification should be easier.

Ryan had rushed Mia away from the gruesome sight and escorted her into the lodge to clean up, while he returned to the porch and hosed off Bandit. That's when he found a gash running along Bandit's side. The poor little guy must have been hit by falling debris. The cut wasn't bleeding heavily so Ryan sat in the rocker on the porch, cradling Bandit to keep him comfortable until Mia settled down and he felt comfortable in leaving her alone to take Bandit to the vet.

The door to the lodge groaned open. Ryan swiveled in his chair and watched Mia exit. She'd changed into blue jeans and an orange hooded sweatshirt from Oregon State University. Her hair shone in the fading sunlight but her red-rimmed eyes held a haunted look that clenched his stomach.

Father, let Mia know you are watching over her and waiting to help her through this tragedy.

He stood, setting Bandit gently on the floor. Bandit slunk under the chair and curled into a ball. Ryan would have turned back and held the pup but Mia needed him more.

He crossed over to her. "You don't look so good."

She shook her head and started to cry softly.

Man. He'd put his foot in his mouth for sure. His heart aching, he pulled her into his arms and held her close. The fresh scent of her apricot shampoo tugged at his senses.

Why hadn't he grabbed her and dragged her away before she saw the body? Since she'd arrived back here, he'd come up short when she needed help the most.

"Isn't this touching," Russ called from the stairs. "Guess you two are back together."

Mia jerked free and scowled at Russ.

Ryan gave his brother a stern glare. "She's upset man. She just found a dead body. Give her a break."

Russ did have the decency to look sheepish.

"So, Mia, I need to hear in your own words what happened."

Her eyes lost their anger and filled with pain. She seemed to freeze in place, unable to speak.

Ryan took her hand and urged her toward the chairs. "Let's sit down."

She dropped down as if it was too much effort to stand.

Ryan retrieved Bandit and held him while she launched into her story, spilling it along with fresh tears. She ended with telling him about the missing locks.

Russ shook his head. "This is just what I thought might happen with that wall. That's why we cordoned it off. What about that yellow tape didn't you understand?"

"Stop complaining," she snapped back. "Thanks to me the firefighters won't have to do the work."

Russ settled on the porch railing and removed his hat to massage his forehead. "Don't pat yourself on the back just yet. They'd have dropped the wall away from the barn to prevent contamination of potential evidence."

Mia's eyes flashed a warning, but Russ didn't notice the fact that she was ready to let him have it. Or maybe he was looking for a good fight.

Ryan held his hand between them. "We could argue about this all day, and it's not going to get us anywhere. There's a body out there, and we need to figure out who it is and why he was killed."

"No 'we' in this, bro. I'll take care of the investigation. You take care of counseling kids." Russ stood and headed for the steps. "I'll call if I need more information."

"Wait." Mia jumped to her feet. "Do you know who it is…in the barn? Or how he died?"

Russ turned. "The ME's preliminary finding suggests blunt force trauma to the head. Once his exam is complete we'll search the body for ID."

"But this is probably the reason for the fire, right?" Mia's gaze hunted around as if she was trying to come up with a reply. "If I hadn't come along when I did the fire would likely have burned the entire barn, and we may never have known a body was there at all."

Ryan hated to disagree with Mia's logic when she was so fragile but as a trained firefighter, he knew her interpretation was off base. He stood and gazed into her eyes. "If the intent of the fire was to do away with the body, it seems likely the arsonist would have started the blaze near the body. And he wouldn't have said he was trying to scare someone off."

Her eyes widened. "So are you saying the fire and the murder aren't related?"

He nodded. "It's possible that the arsonist just wasn't very good at his job."

Russ smiled, but the strain of the gruesome discovery hung around his eyes. "Your theory doesn't take into account the missing locks. Makes sense that the doors were locked to conceal the body, but if the arsonist had a key, that changes things. Once we ID the victim, we should have a better idea on how to proceed."

"I don't suppose anyone in the area has been reported missing?" Ryan asked.

"Not that simple, bro." Russ headed down the stairs. "I'll be in touch."

Ryan watched Mia as she settled back and let her gaze follow Russ. A fierce determination gleamed in her eyes. Somehow, they all found themselves in the middle of a murder investigation, and she was too stubborn to sit on the sidelines and wait for Russ to solve it.

Mia slouched in the overstuffed sofa in front of the fireplace and set the empty teacup on the table. Ryan had prepared tea after coming back from taking Bandit to the vet. Her little puppy came home with ten stitches and a cone over his head to keep him from licking the wound. He curled the best he could on a rug in front of the fire, but he looked so pitiful.

She turned her face to the crackling fire and warmth slid over her body making her drowsy. Her eyes drifted to Ryan who stood next to the window talking on his cell. His face was illuminated by the fading sun, casting shadows on his cheek. They'd decided dinner with David would go on as scheduled so Ryan had stopped at home to change for dinner, and the lemony-yellow sweater left him looking darkly handsome and intriguing.

While he was gone, she'd slipped into black dress pants and a shimmery blouse, and donned her favorite heels. She hoped dressing up might cheer her up. And it had a bit. At least it gave her time to think about how supportive Ryan was being again. He might have repeatedly tried to control her, but knowing about Cara helped Mia understand his motives.

He punched the button on his cell and slid it into his pocket. "That was Russ. They didn't find a wallet on the body. The medical examiner says he's been dead about a week so visual identification won't be easy, either." Ryan crossed the room. "I'm not sure I'm prepared to deal with finding out who was killed." His eyes met hers. "And I can't stand the thought that whoever killed the guy could be after you."

As he settled next to her on the sofa with a deep sigh, flickering flames from the fireplace glimmered off his face, accentuating the crevices of fatigue etched deep into his bronzed skin. His eyes searched hers and the warm intimacy of the moment stole her breath.

Could she hold out against his charms much longer? Did she want to? How could she think this compassionate man would hurt her again?

With gentle fingers, she smoothed the strain from his forehead and trailed a finger down his cheek.

He leaned his face into her hand. His breath whispered over her skin as he exhaled. "When I think about you stuck in that door with the body so close by, I can hardly breathe." He laced his large fingers with her smaller ones and laid them on his knee. "What if you'd found the body when Jessie was with you? The both of you might never have recovered."

Mia shivered, moved closer to Ryan and concentrated on the musky cologne he'd applied when he'd changed for dinner. The scent melded with him and drew her to him. She looked at their hands, so perfectly fitted. Maybe this was how it should be. The two of them together again.

Eyes locked on hers, Ryan tugged on her hand, easing her closer. Her resolve melted away. So what if he'd hurt her once? He was a teenager then. He was an adult now, and he wouldn't do the same thing again.

Could she trust him?

Not when his nearness and compassion were drawing her into making a decision she wasn't ready to make. She needed to put distance between them before she did something stupid.

She pulled her hand free and rose to her feet. "I asked Verna to file an insurance claim yesterday, but she didn't have a real sense of urgency," Mia said, using the first excuse she could find to leave. "I'll go down to the office and see if she did it."

Ryan let out a rasping sigh and came to the edge of the seat. "I'll go with you."

"No. Relax. I'm sure Russ and his men are still at the barn and I'll be safe." Mia started for the door.

His jaw tightened. "It's nearly dark. I don't want you out there alone."

Bandit hopped up, a hopeful gleam in his eyes.

"I'll take Bandit." She lifted his leash off the table. "You'll guard me, won't you, fella," she said to the tail-wagging puppy.

"Still, I'll come with you."

She sighed and snapped the lead on to Bandit's collar. "You can't be with me twenty-four hours a day, Ryan. Nothing is going to happen. I have my cell and Bandit. So chill. I'll be back in a flash and then we can go to David's house."

She pulled the door open and rushed out before Ryan insisted on coming after her. Leaning against a post, she drew in the cooling air to clear her head of his scent and intoxicating gaze. This had to stop. Either she needed to make sure they weren't alone again or she'd find herself running as she'd done since she arrived here. Running into the dark and maybe running for her life if she wasn't careful.

Ryan came to his feet and strode to the front window. If Mia thought he was going to let her traipse off with a miniature dog as her only protection, she was as crazy as he was starting to feel. Lunatic crazy from her waffling behavior.

One minute she was stroking his face, the next she was bolting from him as if he were the killer. He couldn't take much more of it before he sat her down and forced her to tell him what she was thinking. But what good would that do? She never responded well to force.

He peered out the curtains and when she'd gone down the stairs, he counted to ten and went after her. He didn't want to get too close, but he fully intended to keep her within his sight.

He set off at a sedentary pace, his eyes fastened on her back. The wind kicked up from the west and whistled through rasping branches raising his uneasiness. Once he crested the hill where he could watch her make the final trek to the office, he pulled out his cell and dialed Russ.

"I don't have any more news, if that's why you're calling," his brother barked into the phone.

Ryan didn't have a chance with Russ in this kind of mood, but still he had to ask. "Can you post someone at the lodge for the night? I'm really worried something will happen to Mia."

"Don't have enough men the way it is. With no attempt on her life, I can't justify the cost of overtime."

"Cost?" Ryan shouted, the sound traveling down the hill and halting Mia's steps for a moment. She looked back, and he slipped behind a tree and lowered his voice. "Can you put a price on her life?"

"Look. With all the police presence out here today,

it's not likely anyone would go after her tonight. Now if that's all, I have a killer to catch."

"Thanks for nothing." Ryan hung up and watched Mia enter the office.

Father, help me to keep Mia from rushing into danger and work on Russ's heart so he'll offer protection for her.

He rushed down the hill to wait outside until she was finished. Russ said it wasn't likely someone would come after her. Well, Ryan wasn't about to risk her life on an assumption, even if he had to dog her every step.

Mia found Verna sitting with slumped shoulders behind her desk. She wore large glasses with thick lenses and fed papers into a shredder. The very shredder Verna had purchased yesterday and wasn't important to Mia at the time, raised a red flag now.

Mia shut the door and the other woman jumped.

Verna spun her chair. "'Bout scared the living daylights out of me." She slipped a file under a large blotter and glared at Bandit who lunged at the filing cabinet behind the desk. Nose to the floor as best the cone allowed, he sniffed at the bottom drawer.

Verna kept her eyes on him as if afraid of dogs. "When Wally was alive, that dog wasn't allowed in the office."

Mia shushed Bandit, and he settled on his hind legs. She needed to get her questioning over before

Bandit took aim at Verna. "I just stopped by to see if you had a chance to file the insurance claim."

She jutted out her chin. "No, I didn't have time."

Though Mia was taken aback by the virulent response, she shrugged as if it didn't matter. "No problem. I'll take the paperwork with me and fill it out tonight."

Verna didn't move, but sat like a queen on her throne, drumming her fingers on her jean-clad knees.

"Is there a problem with me doing it?" Mia asked.

"Problem? No. I just don't like you inferring I'm incompetent."

Mia waved a hand. "Nothing like that at all. I want to be sure it's done soon, and I know how busy you are." Bandit slowly eased toward the corner cabinet, sniffing the floor on the way. "So is the file in there?"

Verna gave a terse nod.

Mia laughed and tried to lighten the mood. "The way he's acting you must have food stored in there, too."

"Not that it's any of your business, but no." She lifted a key on a chain from around her neck and slid forward to open the top drawer.

Bandit charged on his oversize puppy paws. He rose up on hind legs and sniffed the bottom drawer. If Verna didn't keep food in the cabinet, why would Bandit be all fired crazy about getting in?

Bandit sensed something Mia didn't, but she aimed to find out what. "Glad to see you're careful with the records."

"Never had to do this before, but with all that's been happening since you showed up, I decided it was a good idea to start securing the payroll and tax records."

"That all you keep in there?"

Verna eyed Mia. "Why all the questions?"

Mia shrugged and decided to move on before alerting Verna even more. "Speaking of locking, did you think any more about the barn?"

Verna started thumbing through the files. "Like I said yesterday, there was nothing in there worth locking up so I didn't think about it again."

"Maybe a dead body was reason enough to chain the doors?"

Verna jerked out a folder and slapped it on the desktop. "You aren't gonna shock me that easily, Mia. Russ Morgan told me all about the body." Her eyes held a spark of victory. "Besides, if the guy was already dead there'd be no need to lock him up."

"You're assuming he was dead and in the barn when the chains were put on. Know something I don't?"

She slammed the drawer closed, turned the key then spun with an angry glare burning into Mia's eyes. "I don't like the tone of your voice, young lady. If you've got something to say, come right out and say it—or leave it alone."

As much as Verna was acting all secretive and weird, Mia really didn't think the woman was a murderer. A control freak, a pain in the rear, but not a murderer. It just didn't make sense that she had anything to do with the crimes. She really had no reason to burn down the barn. Besides, the man said he wanted to scare her away and Verna gained nothing by scaring Mia off. If Mia ran, the property went to David, not Verna.

Mia thought it best to end their conversation. "I'll just take the paperwork and go."

Verna thrust the folder at Mia then turned her back.

Mia tugged on Bandit's leash and rushed into the darkened outdoors where the temperature had turned as frosty as Verna's attitude. Ryan stood by the door, clapping his arms to keep warm.

"Are you okay?" His eyes searched her body as if looking for injury.

Her heart melted over his concern, but her rational brain was irritated from his need to watch her every move. "What are you doing out here? I feel like you're stalking me."

"I want to make sure you're safe." His words reverberated with concern.

With a tone like that, she couldn't be mad at him, but she wasn't going to let him pull her in with some deep conversation like in the lodge.

She'd keep things light between them. "As stalkers go, you're bearable."

He rewarded her acquiescence with a dynamic smile. "Let's get this little guy settled in his crate so we're not late for dinner."

She tugged on Bandit's leash to get him moving in the right direction. Ryan fell into step with her. A ruffling noise sounded ahead on the path. Bandit shot off, dragging Mia behind.

She jogged with him until he reached the porch and paused at the bottom of the steps.

"Wonder what spooked him?" Ryan let his gaze rove over the area.

"Probably some animal."

"Or not." He stopped and let his eyes connect with hers. "In the future, Mia, I don't want you out here alone. Especially not in the dark."

She bristled at his demanding tone. "Don't worry about me. I'll be fine." Her words had been strong, but as she looked at the bullet holes in the door, uncertainty constricted her heart.

Would she be fine or would the person behind all these threats strike again? Not with a warning, but this time with a deadly attack.

FIFTEEN

Mia fixed a smile on her face and listened to David's family engage in good-humored teasing. This was the way of life she remembered before their mother died. The way of life she longed for again. The life she could have if she would let go of the pain and demands inflicted by her father. And of course, if she could find a man she could trust not to take over her life and smother her.

She looked at Ryan, her heart warming at how he'd jumped in when nerves had her stammering answers to questions. He'd playfully tickled both of the girls, chatted easily with Peg and David while Mia sat frozen on the sofa unable to relax and interact. The stakes were so high here. Alone after Uncle Wally's death, she needed family and she didn't want to do anything to jeopardize a relationship that might be forming.

Ryan crossed the space and sat next to her. "Relax," he whispered. "You're a pretty terrific woman. Just be yourself and they can't help but love you."

Her eyes met his and a heavy weight lifted from

her shoulders. He was the real deal. Everything he professed to be. A strong man, yet one with compassion and kindness. A man who had her best interest in heart. A man she should give in to and trust.

Hanna, David's six-year-old daughter, came across the room and stood before Mia, breaking the spell between her and Ryan.

Hanna fingered Mia's wispy blouse. "When I grow up I'm gonna wear pretty clothes like these everyday."

Mia offered a genuine smile. "I like to dress up, too."

"Do you wanna see my party dresses?"

"Hanna," David warned. "Mia's here to visit with all of us."

Hanna's lips turned down.

"How about we take a really quick look?" Mia asked.

"Yay!" Hanna shouted, and tugged Mia from the couch.

Mia let Hanna lead her up a winding staircase to a pink frilly bedroom. Hanna jabbered about parties, dresses and shoes while Mia nodded and offered affirmation when appropriate.

Hanna held out a pair of black patent dress shoes. "Grandpa gave me these shoes for my birthday. They even have heels like yours."

Mia's cheerful mood evaporated. She kept her smile fixed in place but her stomach turned. Would she ever be able to think about her father without this pain or was she deluding herself? Had she really ruined any chance to repair the rift with him after blaming him for the fire?

The doorbell chimed, and Hanna jumped to her feet. "Let's go see who's here." She raced out of the room, leaving Mia to follow.

At the landing, she heard Hanna shriek, "Grandpa!"

Mia paused, her nervous butterflies returning.

Male voices she recognized as her father's and David's drifted up the steps.

"Did she come?" her father asked.

"Yes, but before you go in, you need to know I didn't tell her you'd be here."

"Surprising her like this isn't a good idea, David."

"I didn't think she would come if she knew you'd be here and this has to stop before it escalates any further. I for one don't want another visit from the police asking me if I'm involved in a crime, do you?"

"No, that was humiliating to say the least." He sighed.

So this is why he came. Because he'd been embarrassed. Mia's heart tightened, sending a pain into her chest.

"I can understand her thinking badly of me. I deserve it," her father continued. "People she's run into since she's been back tell me what a fine woman she's turned out to be, and I can't reconcile that with her sending Russ to interrogate me."

"She didn't…I did." Ryan's voice, sure and strong floated up to Mia.

Surprised that Ryan joined the other men, she crept closer so she could see the trio.

"I don't understand," her father said.

"You never have." The anger in Ryan's tone touched Mia's heart. "Even though the two of you have the only valid motives to want her gone, she would never ask Russ to talk to you. Even when Russ blamed her for the terrible things going on around here."

"Russ thinks Mia is involved in all this?" David's tone suggested he was shocked.

"Not anymore." Ryan ran a hand over his head. "Look. We're here for a nice dinner. What say for one night we forget the past and try to get to know the incredible woman Mia has turned out to be? You owe her at least that much."

Tears at Ryan's kindness threatened to break free. True, he was taking charge, making things happen on his timeframe and in his way, but she could see this time it was done out of pure compassion.

She swiped a thumb under her eyes, and headed for the stairs. No matter how her father and David answered Ryan's request, she would not hide from them anymore.

After dinner, Ryan held the door of his truck and Mia climbed in. He was amazed at how well the evening turned out. He didn't know when Mia had decided to give her father a chance but she had. Sure, their dinnertime conversations were filled with stilted meaningless chitchat and hard to watch, but Ryan saw the desire in both of them to find common ground.

Feeling like whistling over the success of the evening, he ran to the other side of the truck and climbed in. He cautioned himself to cool it. Quit pushing as hard as he had in the last few days and let her choose the topic of their conversation.

He slipped the truck into gear and eased on to the highway. They rode in silence for several miles before she started to fiddle with the handle on a gadget bag sitting on the seat between them.

"Have you taken up photography?" she asked almost as if she didn't know she was speaking.

"Me? Nah. Chuck borrowed my truck to get supplies for the documentary crew and left this stuff in here."

"Hope he doesn't mind if I snoop." She zipped open the bag and pulled out a camera. "He must have dropped a bundle on this."

"I forgot you were into photography. You do any of that anymore?"

"Not much since high school. I still keep up to date on cameras, though. Would love to have a digital SLR, but this one is around two grand for just the body."

Ryan laughed. "SLR? In English, please."

"Oh, sorry. SLR is single lens reflex."

"Right. *Much* better explanation." He laughed again.

She held the camera up and looked out the window. "Maybe when I get back to Atlanta I should take this up again."

Get back to Atlanta. She said it with great enthusiasm, as if this was the best present she could receive. Not for him. He hated the idea of her leaving. They'd just started to get to know each other again. If the creep threatening her was caught, the two of them could settle into a nice routine. As friends. Maybe more. Once she was safe, out of danger so he didn't need to worry about losing her.

But what if her heart wasn't free? What if she had someone in Atlanta and that was behind her desire to return?

He didn't want to spoil the mood, but he had to ask. "You sound so eager to go back home. Is there a boyfriend waiting for you there?"

"No one special." Her tone was laced with a hint of melancholy, and she ended with a sigh.

Maybe she *was* free. "I'm surprised no man has snapped you up by now."

She shrugged. "It's not easy finding someone you want to spend the rest of your life with."

"Or keeping them," he said in whisper that sent all of his pain at losing Cara into the space.

Mia settled the camera on her lap and faced him. "Gladys told me what happened with your fiancée.

I'm so sorry for your loss. That must have been terrible for you."

"Thank you. Lots of people have said that to me over the last few years, but I've wondered if they understood." He flipped on the blinker to signal his turn into Pinetree's driveway. "With the loss of your mother, you're one person who knows how I feel." Making the turn, he shook his head. "I should have been there for Cara."

Mia squeezed his arm. "Blaming yourself for what happened is a heavy burden to carry, Ryan. Take it from me. No matter what happened, you weren't at fault. You didn't kill her. You need to let it go or you'll never be able to develop a relationship with another woman."

"No worries there. I'll never risk getting hurt like that again." The bitterness in his tone closed down the conversation.

Without comment, Mia lifted the camera to the window and peered through the viewfinder.

Just as well. He didn't want to talk about it. Especially as the inky darkness broken only by his headlights seemed to shout out to protect Mia from future danger. Either Russ and his team had finished processing the murder scene or they'd gone home to return in the light of day. Ryan hoped they'd found a lead to move this investigation forward.

"Did you see that?" Mia's tone tingled with excitement.

"What?"

She pointed toward the resort office. "Over there. A light flashed in the window." She rubbed her eyes and stared. "There it is again. Like a flashlight."

He slowed the truck and followed the line of her finger. "Yeah. You think someone broke in?"

"Maybe Verna's working late."

"With a flashlight? Not likely." He flipped off the headlights, checked the office and watched the light cutting through the room. "This could have something to do with the threats."

Mia sat forward and kept the camera trained on the office. The lens whirred out. "This has got a great zoom, but I still can't make out who's in there."

"Let's get closer for a better look." He turned off the engine. "I'll coast down the hill so we don't draw attention to ourselves."

With the engine dead, chirping crickets filled the void as did the crunching of tires over gravel. He let inertia pull the truck closer, and near the store he swung the wheel hard to the left taking them as close to the building as he dare without being seen.

He turned to Mia. "See anything?"

"We're not at the right angle." She grabbed the door handle.

"Oh, no, you don't," he said and reached up to flip off the dome light. "I'll go check. You wait here."

"Are you kidding me? I'm coming with you." She raced outside before he could stop her impulsive action.

He joined her near the front bumper. "I don't want

you to get hurt, but I know I can't stop you. Humor me and at least stay behind me. Okay?"

"Okay." She fell into place behind him.

Grateful for her easy acquiescence, he led the way as they crept to the long narrow porch running the length of the office and small convenience store. He signaled for her to stay put while he looked into the window. Surprisingly, she agreed again. Maybe she was learning to trust him.

With silent footfalls, he closed the distance to the window and slowly rose up to look.

What?

Someone was in the office all right, but it wasn't Verna as Mia suggested. Someone, with a flashlight in hand, was trying to break into the file cabinet. Ryan couldn't make out clear details, but he could see enough to know this was a bulky, tall male, who didn't appear to be armed.

What should they do? This had to be related to the fire, maybe even Mia's bracelet and the murder. If it was, they couldn't let the guy get away.

Ryan eased back from the window and joined Mia. "It's a man, breaking into the file cabinet," he whispered. "We need to call Russ."

"It'll take too long for him to get here. This guy could get away."

"We'll sit right here. If he tries to leave before Russ arrives, we'll think of something."

Mia nodded and Ryan made the call while they settled on the bottom step to wait.

Time ticked by in slow increments, palpable tension enveloping them.

Mia shivered, and he wrapped an arm around her. She looked up at him with a confidence he didn't like glinting in her eyes.

"My turn to go look," she whispered.

He took her hand. "Wait for Russ."

She shook her hand free. "No. We have to see what this guy's up to."

"Fine. Then I'll go." Ryan moved before she could stop him. At the window, he raised up like a peeping tom. The man had already wrenched open the file cabinet lock and held a cloth bag filled with files.

That was odd. Of all the valuable equipment in the room, why take files?

Mia sneezed, breaking the silence. The man spun and started toward the door.

Ryan dropped down and frantically signaled that the intruder was on his way out, and Mia needed to get out of the doorway.

Instead of moving away, she stood and planted her legs wide. Ryan heard a whirring sound coming from the camera.

"Close your eyes," Mia whispered.

"What for?" Ryan asked.

The door wrenched open.

Mia fired off picture after picture.

"What the—" the man shouted.

Ryan clenched his eyes from the flash's bright light. He got it now. She was trying to blind the guy so he couldn't leave. Too bad Ryan hadn't taken her advice and closed his eyes. He rubbed his eyes and listened. He heard the guy banging around as if he were dazed.

Footfalls traveled past Ryan. The flashes should have rendered this man's eyesight as useless as his eyes, but Ryan wouldn't take any chances. Hoping to tackle the intruder, he shot from his spot. Missed him. Banged his shoulder into the porch post.

"Think something that stupid will stop me, girly," the gruff voice shouted from an area that sounded very near Mia.

Ryan blinked hard. Through the splotches coloring his vision he saw the huge male body slam into her.

"No!" he shouted and leapt to his feet.

Mia hit the ground hard. Her head snapped back. The camera catapulted into the air.

"Stop," Ryan commanded and bolted down the stairs.

The intruder uttered a foul laugh before charging into the darkness. Ryan wanted to chase after him, but needed to check Mia.

Please, Lord, let her be all right.

He turned and knelt by her unmoving body. "Are you okay?"

She slowly sat and looked around. "What happened to the camera? Chuck's gonna kill me if I broke it."

Ryan sat back on his haunches and laughed out his

tension. Her ability to stay levelheaded when under fire was one of the things he'd always liked about her.

Thank you, God, for protecting her.

"We might be able to catch that guy. Do you think we should go after him?" She'd survived an attack and seemed determined to come to the bottom of what happened, not run away in fright.

His smile fell away. This was too similar to Cara. She'd said she could handle that creep Quentin. Said he deserved for her to continue counseling him even when he'd formed an unhealthy affection for her. Now, Mia, who God help him, he'd started to care about more than he should, wanted to chase the man who'd slammed her on to the concrete.

He prayed for the strength and wisdom to keep her safe.

SIXTEEN

If Mia believed God looked out for her, she would thank Him for saving her life right now. More likely, He was looking out for Ryan who'd survived the intruder's escape without injury. She was not so lucky. The back of her head throbbed. She gingerly felt the area and winced. Her fingers came away sticky. Blood. She swiveled on her bottom and spotted the concrete parking block where she'd hit her head.

No way she'd tell Ryan about the blood. He'd return to clucking over her like a mother hen. Although she was beginning to warm to his concern and wouldn't mind if he pulled her into his arms and comforted her, she wanted to get into the office and see what the burglar had done before Russ arrived and took over the crime scene. If Ryan knew she was bleeding he would make her see a doctor.

Mia rocked forward, trying to get up. Dizziness enveloped her. She sat back.

"Here." Ryan handed her the camera. "Let me help you." He bent low and lifted her by the arm.

She lurched to her feet and swayed.

"Whoa." He grabbed her by the upper arms. "Are you sure you're okay?"

"Fine, just got the air knocked out of me." Mia pointed down the driveway for a diversion. "Looks like Russ is here."

She'd expected Russ to come barreling down the drive with lights blaring, but then he didn't know the burglar had run off and Russ was likely in stealth mode so he could catch him.

"Can you wait here for Russ while I take a quick look to see what was stolen?" She didn't wait for an answer, but started moving toward the office as fast as she could before fresh waves of dizziness took her down.

In the office, she found the tall file cabinet behind Verna's desk tipped on the side. Files splayed across the linoleum like avalanched snow. A filled white pillowcase sat near the files.

She wanted to peek in the case, but Russ and Ryan's voices drifted through the doorway stopping her. Russ would come inside soon, and she didn't want him to catch her touching anything.

Her back to the door, she took in every detail. The computer, other office equipment and valuables were untouched. This guy wasn't a random thief. He wanted information. If they hadn't interrupted him, he would probably have gone for the computer hard drive next.

Too bad he'd worn a cap pulled low over his eyes,

and in the dark she hadn't seen him clearly or she could at least have given Russ a description of the guy.

"You're hurt," Ryan said from behind.

She jumped and spun around to face him.

He stood in the doorway, alone. She could hear Russ talking outside. Maybe one of his officers had also arrived.

Eyes flashing with worry, Ryan strode across the room. "Why didn't you tell me you were bleeding?"

"Because I wanted to get a look inside before Russ got here and sent me packing."

"Let me look at it." He turned her around, and she wobbled. "Dizziness is not a good sign." He softly probed with his fingers. "The wound doesn't look too bad. Are you nauseous?"

She faced him and smiled. "No, I'm fine. Just a bump."

His eyes creased, and his mouth drew up in a pucker. "You don't appear to have a concussion, but I think you should have it checked out anyway."

She waved away his concern. "Really, I'm fine. But thanks."

"If you won't go to the doctor, you'll need someone to check on you tonight. To make sure you really are okay."

"I think you're overreacting."

"And I think you're downplaying how serious this

could be." He stroked the side of her face, letting his fingers linger long enough to raise her heartbeat.

Even if he was trying to take charge, she enjoyed the feel of his fingers. Coarse yet gentle against her skin.

"You two better not have touched anything." Russ charged inside, an officer trailing on his heels. He looked at Mia. "Can you tell what's missing?"

Ryan hissed out a breath and removed his hand. "You done with me, bro?"

"You can go."

What? Ryan was so concerned and now he was going to abandon her when the great inquisitor had entered the room?

Ryan pulled out his cell. "I need to update my staff in case the burglar is still on the property." He looked into Mia's eyes. "Anything I can do for you?"

He wasn't deserting her. The warmth oozing from his eyes settled over her like an electric blanket.

Russ gave a pointed cough. "You two lovebirds about done so I can ask Mia a few questions?"

Lovebirds? Russ must be mistaken. Mia looked at Ryan and at his intense gaze she felt a rush of heat shoot up her neck.

He laughed at her discomfort, obviously not bothered by this public display of affection. "I'll go check out the lodge to be sure this guy didn't make a stop in there first."

"Good idea," Russ said. "Report back if you find a problem."

Ryan went outside, dialing his cell as he went.

Mia, feeling her face start to cool, crossed the room. Now that Ryan was gone, she didn't need to keep up the pretense of feeling fine. "Would it be okay if I sat while we talked?"

"Fine by me," Russ said.

Mia gently lowered her battered body on to the cracked vinyl chair by Verna's desk and put aside the emotions Ryan had stirred up to concentrate on the break-in.

"Can you tell what's missing?" Russ asked.

She described what she'd observed then launched into her take on the burglary. Russ interrupted frequently to ask clarifying questions, making the process take forever. His questions went on and on, eating up time Mia could better use to figure out who'd broken into the office.

Thirty minutes after he began, he abruptly ended by stabbing his finger at her lap. "That the camera?"

She lifted the mangled body. "It is."

"If I remember right you're a photography buff. Any hope we can get a picture of the guy off that?"

"Depends. If the flash was bright enough and if the memory card is still intact then maybe." She tried to open the small compartment housing the memory card. "I can't get it out, but maybe Chuck can remove it without damaging the card."

"Who's Chuck?"

"A photographer on the documentary crew and the camera's owner."

Russ nodded as if for the first time she answered his question correctly. "Good idea. Normally, I'd take the camera into evidence and get the state lab to extract the card, but breaking and entering is such a minor offense the lab will take their sweet time. You think you can get this Chuck guy to work on it right away?"

"I'll ask."

"Let me know if he can't fit it in soon, and I'll get one of my men to send it in. Before I let you go, let's take a look in that pillowcase to see if the contents mean anything to you." Snapping on latex gloves, he crossed the room and lifted the case onto Verna's desk.

"It's full of files." He drew out a stack of manila folders and then handed her a pair of gloves. "Check these out. Anything significant?"

Mia set down the camera then donned the gloves and flipped through the stack. "They're financial records for Pinetree, but I can't see why someone would want to steal them."

He gave her a clipped nod. "I'll get Verna's take on them tomorrow."

The idea of Verna looking at these didn't sit well with Mia. If the property manager was up to something, she could hide the evidence or just not explain what the documents held. "I think you'd get a better evaluation from Kurt Loomis. He handles the finances for Pinetree."

Russ's scowl lightened. "Thanks for the tip." He cleared his throat as if saying thanks made him uncomfortable. "I need to help my officer so you're free to go."

Mia was tempted to comment on his discomfort, but shed her gloves then picked up the camera and exited with her mouth closed. Russ clomped behind. Outside, the air had chilled considerably, and Mia wrapped her arms around her stomach to chase away the cold.

Russ came alongside her and made a quick jerk of his head at the lodge. "Looks like your Prince Charming is on his way back."

She ignored his sarcasm and waited for Ryan who clipped along the path with a flashlight illuminating his way. Her face warmed at the memory of his parting gaze. She hated to admit it, but she hoped he'd look at her the same way when he arrived.

How hopeless was she? Less than an hour ago he'd told her he didn't want to care about a woman ever again and she had her own emotional baggage preventing her from moving forward with him. And still she wanted him to be interested in her…?

Wishing she could let go and trust him, she watched him amble down the path. When he got nearer, she could see the outline of Bandit's cone as he leapt and snapped at the moving beam. He caught her scent and charged. She wanted to bend down and greet him, but her head was still woozy.

Not that it mattered. He galloped straight past her and into the office.

Russ grunted. "Guess you haven't learned to control him, huh?"

"Let's see. How many hours have I had free for dog training?"

"Mia, where are your manners?" Gladys, wearing a faded caftan with bat-like arms and cinched around her waist, stepped out from behind Ryan.

"What are you doing here?" Mia asked.

Ryan stepped forward. "I called her. Since you won't go to the doctor, someone has to check on you throughout the night."

Mia flashed him a frustrated glare.

Gladys tromped between them and snatched the flashlight out of Ryan's hand. With her tongue poking from the side of her mouth, she came at Mia. She used her finger to probe the bump on Mia's scalp as the flashlight warmed the skin. "You're right, Ryan. Doesn't appear to need stitches." She turned to Ryan. "I can take care of things now."

"Don't leave that dog here," Russ said with a scowl.

"I'll get him." Ryan came toward the office.

Before he reached the sagging porch, Bandit charged out. He paused to look up at Mia. She laughed at the crazy expression on his face surrounded by the plastic cone. His mouth clenched around something thick, small and brown, and she sobered.

"Do you see that?" Russ asked. "What in the world does he have?"

"Bandit," Mia called in singsong. "Come here, boy. Let me see."

So as not to scare him, she eased closer. He wagged his little tail as if he was excited to see her then shot into the darkness.

"You better hope he didn't take anything important," Russ said.

Mia waved off Russ. "Relax. He probably just swiped a treat from the store."

"Let me know what happens with that camera," Russ said over his shoulder as he went to join the other officer at his car.

"Okay," Gladys slipped her hand under Mia's elbow. "Let's get you up to the lodge."

"I need to talk to Russ about something then I'll stop in to make sure you're settled." Ryan patted Mia's arm.

For once, Mia didn't argue. She let Gladys lead her away without complaint, because she knew Ryan had her best interests at heart.

She appreciated his concern for her safety—and she didn't want to do anything to cause him more pain—but no matter his fear she couldn't be coddled. She'd go to the lodge now, but she had no intention of simply sitting around and waiting for another attack.

* * *

Ryan let the worry he'd kept in check in Mia's presence whoosh out in a large breath. Using a flashlight, he looked at the concrete where she'd hit her head. A large splotch darkened one side.

Mia's blood.

Terror shot into his chest.

He cared for her. How much he didn't know, but she'd become important to him again. Without God's grace, she might have been hurt much worse.

Ryan had been powerless to help her. This couldn't happen again. He couldn't lose her. He had to protect her. This time he wouldn't let Russ turn down his request.

"Hey, bro," he called out to slow Russ on one of his trips into the office. "I need to talk to you about something."

Russ stopped. "Make it fast. I've got a lot of work to do."

Ryan joined him. "Earlier you said you wouldn't put a man out here to watch Mia, but things have changed. You have to admit with what just happened, she's in real danger."

"She wouldn't have gotten hurt if the two of you had waited for me to arrive." Russ tossed an extension cord to his officer.

Ryan clenched his fists. He opened his mouth to let his brother have it, but Russ continued. "We'll probably be here most of the night so she should be fine. I'll check the duty roster tomorrow and see if I can do anything." Russ looked down as if he didn't want to see Ryan's gratitude. "That all?"

"Yeah, go back to tormenting your rookie."

Russ laughed and grabbed a box from the hood of his car.

Weary, Ryan hopped into his truck and drove the short distance to the lodge.

Gladys answered the door, flinging it wide. "Good, now you can tell Mia it's foolish to go out looking for that dog after all she's been through."

"Bandit?" Ryan asked. "Didn't he come back here?"

"No…and Mia's worried to death over the little thing. I've got her all cleaned up and she should rest, not go tromping in the woods at night."

Ryan pushed past Gladys and looked for Mia so he could reinforce Gladys's point of view. "Where is she?"

"In the bedroom putting her boots on." Gladys clutched his arm. "You will stop her, won't you?"

Would he be able to talk some sense into her for once? Not likely. But that wouldn't stop him from attempting it. "I'll try, Gladys, but you know how stubborn she can be."

"Don't I ever," Gladys spit out. "She hasn't even looked at the DVD I gave her. She thinks it's a waste of time."

Ryan didn't have the heart to tell Gladys he thought the same thing. "She's been busy."

Gladys crossed her arms. "Well, she has time

tonight. I put it in her laptop and loaded the file. Next time she checks her e-mail it'll be open and waiting. It's for her own good, you know."

"Whose good?" Mia asked as she strolled into the room.

"Never you mind." Gladys toddled over to Mia. "Now why don't you sit down, and I'll make a cup of tea."

Mia shook her head, setting the wet tendrils of her hair slapping her shoulders. "First I'm going to look for Bandit."

Gladys jabbed Ryan in the ribs.

He rubbed the ache from her punch. "It's not a good idea to go out there. What if the burglar is still hanging around?"

"Are you kidding? With Russ here…not likely." She went to the door and pulled a jacket down from a peg mounted on the wall.

She had a point; the same one Russ made. Ryan really didn't have a good argument to stop her.

"Wait, Mia." Gladys glared at him. "Ryan will go with you."

"I'm a big girl, Gladys," Mia said, her shoulders pulled back. "I can do things without a man."

"Give Gladys a break, Mia. She's just worried about you." Ryan left off the fact that he was also worried for her safety, and he joined her at the door.

"Fine, you can tag along, but don't get in my way."

As Mia exited, he turned back to Gladys. "Go

ahead and get the water boiling for tea. This shouldn't take long."

At least he hoped it wouldn't take long because he wanted to get to the bottom of her snarly attitude before she rushed off into the night like this again.

Shining the flashlight, Mia charged down the stairs and toward a stand of pine trees lining the property. Irritation with Ryan hung on her shoulders like heavy weights.

What was with men anyway? Why did they have to take charge *all* the time?

She reached the edge of the woods and called Bandit's name. A scurrying sound in the trees caught her attention. She checked it out, but found nothing. These woods were full of small nocturnal animals, and her tromping around had upset their nightly routine.

Ryan clasped a hand on her shoulder. "After that head injury, you should take things a little slower."

She counted to ten so her tone would come out less terse. "I don't need you to take over my life and protect me. I can take care of myself." Never mind that she'd not been doing a very good job of it lately.

His eyes darkened. "When are you going to learn accepting help isn't a sign of weakness? Even if the help comes from a man." He said *a man* as if it were poison he was spitting out.

Mia marched off. He rustled behind and stopped

her by the arm, then gently turned her to face him. "Look, I'm sorry if I sounded so mean. I know your father did a number on you, but not all men are the same. Some of us really want to be helpful with no strings attached."

His sincere tone broke through her anger, and she considered his words. Though she hated to admit it, he was right. Through the years, she'd transferred her father's controlling nature on to every man she'd dated or who'd tried to help her except Uncle Wally. She had to find a way to put her father's betrayal and oppressive ways to rest, but that didn't mean she was ready to admit she'd overreacted.

"So, what're you waiting for?" she said, ending with a forced laugh to let him know she'd gotten his point without having to discuss it. "Let's find Bandit."

They searched for the next hour to no avail. Her head pounded and the cool damp air settled into her soul. She was growing more irritable by the minute and knew it was time to call it a night before she snapped at Ryan again. She told him as much and like the perfect gentleman he was turning out to be, he walked her home.

Wanting to end the night on a good note, she rested against the post on the porch to think of how to thank him for his concern without encouraging him to overreact in the future. Maybe she could start with something neutral and ease her way in. "Do you think Bandit will be okay?"

"He's a dog. A night outside won't hurt him."

"What if he runs into a bigger and more powerful animal?" Her voice broke at the end as she thought of her little defenseless friend at the mercy of wild animals.

Ryan climbed the stairs, invading her personal space and coming eye to eye with her. "Why, Mia Blackburn, I think you actually care about something of the male persuasion. Maybe there's hope for me in the future."

Picking up on his light mood, she stabbed her finger in his firm chest. "What? A future? For someone who just told me he never wanted a long-term relationship again, this sounds to me like you're hoping to start one."

He latched on to her finger and pulled her against his chest. His eyes were smoky and irresistible in the shadowed light. "Newsflash, Mia. Women aren't the only ones who can change their minds. I may have found a reason to reconsider."

She opened her mouth to issue a snappy comeback but his lips descended on hers before she could speak. Soft and warm, they melted the cold that had taken hold of her body. She slid her hands over his shoulders and up his neck, past the rough stubble of his jaw. Just as her fingers tickled the ends of his hair, he set her away.

Breathing deep, he traced his finger down the side of her face then leaned close. "I'll see you in the morning," he whispered with his breath tickling her neck.

He jogged down the steps and to his truck. She reached her hand up to touch the spot on her neck and listened to the pebbles ricochet from under his tires.

Had he just asked to pursue a future with her or was he simply flirting? She shook her head and went inside. Didn't matter what his intentions were. She wouldn't get involved with him for the long run.

Problem was, she'd proven she was barely able to resist his tender charms for a few days. So how would she do so for an entire year?

SEVENTEEN

Dressed in her favorite jeans and a soft white T-shirt, Mia was ready for whatever the new day brought. When the sun had shone bright, she'd convinced Gladys she was safe and the overpowering woman went home. Mia was now on the porch calling for Bandit who failed to return.

Hands cupped around her mouth she called several times. As much as she had claimed she was brave, the chilling events of the last day filled her with enough unease that she'd opted not to go off on her own in search of him.

At the sound of her ringing phone, she gave up and ran inside. Maybe Ryan was calling with news about Bandit.

"Hello," she answered in a breathy voice from the run.

"Did I catch you at a bad time?" Kurt Loomis asked.

Disappointed it wasn't Ryan, Mia slipped on to a bar stool and put her brother's business partner at ease. "Not at all."

"Well, I'm glad I caught you. I just spoke to Russ Morgan about the files he dropped off earlier, and I wanted to give you a heads-up before this news hit the grapevine." Kurt sounded worried, but Mia was intrigued more than concerned. "You might not believe this, but the folders hold clear evidence of Verna's embezzlement from Pinetree."

Mia shot to her feet. "Verna stole money?"

"A considerable amount, actually. Not that I had a clue. I spotted a decline in income, but the records showed higher vacancy rates so it seemed normal." The accountant sighed. "I feel kind of stupid for not seeing it, but as the owner, Wally would've been the one to question lower income, not me."

Mia tried to wrap her mind around what this meant. If Verna was embezzling, she might be trying to get rid of Mia before she discovered the crime.

"Did Russ tell you how he was going to proceed?"

"No, but I'd imagine you'll need to press charges before anything can happen."

Mia fought to keep the excitement out of her tone. "Thank you for letting me know, Kurt."

Promising to keep her in the loop as he reviewed additional files, he said goodbye.

So Verna *was* up to something. This certainly explained her odd behavior. Plus she could've had access to the bracelet and would definitely know it would hurt Mia. She could've locked the barn, too. But kill someone? That was too far-fetched. Of course, the murder could be unrelated.

A knock sounded on the door.

Mia crossed the room and peeked out the window. Ryan.

She jerked the door open. "Have I got news for you." She told him about Kurt's call with her words tumbling out like a rushing river. "Where do you think Verna is? Do you think Russ will arrest her? Should we go down to the office and see?"

Ryan clamped his hands on her arms and stilled her anxious fidgeting. "Slow down. Let me think."

She didn't want to wait. She wanted Verna in jail and paying for her crimes. "Verna could be getting away."

"That's a little rash. She doesn't even know Kurt looked at the files." Ryan stroked her arms as if he thought it would appease her, but nothing would stop her now.

"She may not know Kurt looked at them, but she will know they're missing after the break-in. Wait! Why would she have someone break into the office to steal the files?"

He shrugged. "To get rid of the evidence, I guess."

"But she could just take the files. Or shred them. Like she was doing last night before the break-in." Mia clutched Ryan's shirt. "Oh, my gosh! She was destroying evidence right in front of me, and I didn't know it. We have to get down there before she shreds any more."

Mia grabbed her jacket from the peg and rushed out the door without waiting to see if Ryan followed. She headed straight for the John Deere, revved the engine and then turned to see if he was coming.

Face expressing his exasperation, he jogged across the space. "I'm surprised you waited."

"Sorry." She shifted into gear and aimed the vehicle down the driveway. "I'm so happy we've figured this out that I can't wait to get it resolved."

"I'm happy, too, but I think we should talk to Russ first."

Ryan was right, but she'd felt helpless for days. She had to do something—now.

"Did you hear that?" Ryan asked.

"What?"

"A dog barking. Did Bandit ever come home?"

She shook her head and slowed the vehicle to listen. An excited yipping echoed from the north end of the barn.

"Sounds like Bandit. I hope he's okay."

"Shut this thing down, and we'll check." Ryan's voice rang with relief.

She didn't know if he was glad they'd located Bandit, or glad her energy had moved in a different direction. Either way she turned the key and followed him across the lawn and into the soggy muck. They climbed under the restrung crime-scene tape and found Bandit very near the spot where they'd found the body.

Bandit scraped the cone through ashes as he rutted around like a pig. Memories of the gruesome discovery assaulted her brain. No way she wanted to go closer.

"Come here, boy," she called. "You'll get your stitches dirty."

He looked up at her as if he understood then whined and scrounged in the same spot, upping his motions to frantic.

"He's being stubborn," Ryan said.

"Looks more like he's found something and doesn't want to leave it alone." Mia carefully picked her way through the mess.

"I'll get him." Ryan pushed past her, plopping his booted feet into the muck and splattering gunk all about.

As Ryan lifted Bandit from the debris and held the dirty little fella away from his chest, she searched his body for injury. He aimed his tongue at Ryan, but with the cone still circling his neck, the cause was hopeless.

She turned to the spot where Bandit had cleared the rubbish. The tip of a small brown object poked from the ruins.

"That looks like a wallet." Mia retrieved the item and held it up to Ryan.

"A man's wallet. I bet this belongs to the man we

found out here." Ryan locked eyes with her. "Let's get out of this mess and see if it holds any ID."

They retreated to an area of lush lawn free from standing water. She ignored Bandit's frantic squirming, flipped open the wallet and pulled out the driver's license.

Holding the wallet away from her, she gaped at the picture. Her legs turned rubbery, and she dropped to her knees sinking into the thick grass.

How could this be? Another person she loved dead. This one murdered and thrown out like trash.

She sucked in gulps of air as panic ricocheted through her.

"What is it?" Ryan sat next to her.

Bandit wiggled free and yipped at the wallet.

"I know this man." She handed the driver's license to Ryan then rested her chin on her knees.

"Franklin Springer from Dunwoody, Georgia." Ryan looked at Mia. "Did you know him well?"

"We called him Fuzzy. He was Wally's good friend. Kinda like my uncle. In fact, I sat with him at Uncle Wally's funeral." Her voice gave out and tears began to roll down her cheeks. Her head felt heavy, filled with so much pain it might explode.

"I'm so sorry." Ryan wrapped an arm around her shoulder and held her.

She worked hard to control her emotions. She pulled back and peered at him. He wiped her tears with a gentle finger.

He was being so kind. So nice. He'd proven

himself trustworthy. She could get used to turning to him when life kicked her around like this.

But then what? He'd die or betray her again just like everyone else she loved. No way she'd open herself up for that kind of hurt.

She shrugged off his arm and stood. "I don't know why I'm surprised to learn Fuzzy died. This is the kind of thing I've come to expect in my life. Everyone I care about either dies or turns on me."

Ryan pushed to his feet, his eyes contrite. "I'm in no position to say anything about betrayal except to remind you my actions weren't what they seemed at the time."

"I know that now. That means God will have to take you away from me in another way."

"Is that what you really think? That God is causing all of these things to happen to make your life miserable?"

"Don't you?" She let her gaze fall away from his confused eyes. "Right…I forgot. You used to share this opinion with me but that's changed."

"Back then I really didn't know God. Now that I have a relationship with Him, I know He doesn't cause bad things to happen."

"Really? Then why do they happen?" She let sarcasm shoot through her words as she watched Ryan's face, waiting for him to convince her that God was not her enemy.

"This is a tough thing to understand. Even those who have a much deeper walk with God than me struggle with it. But here's how I see it." He came closer and clasped her hands in his. "God doesn't cause bad things to happen, but He allows them to happen for a variety of reasons. For me, it's usually to get my attention and draw me closer to Him."

She pulled her hands free. "That's pretty lame, if you ask me. I did bad things in high school to get my father's attention and that was wrong. So why can God do the same thing and believers think it's a good thing?"

"It's different, Mia. God has a perfect understanding of what's good for us so He knows what to allow. We, on the other hand, don't have a clue what's in our best interest, just what our feelings tell us we want." He paused as if waiting for her to stop him, but she was actually interested in hearing a logical explanation.

"I'm listening."

"One of my favorite verses in the Bible is in Proverbs. Trust in the Lord with all your heart and lean not on your own understanding. If you can trust that everything will ultimately be good for you and not let your feelings color a situation, life will be a lot simpler. Letting God be in charge of my life makes the living so much easier."

"But I like to be in charge so people can't step all over me ever again." The vehemence in her tone shocked her. Was she that bitter about her past?

His lips tipped in a gentle smile meant to comfort.

"And how's that working for you? Are you happy? Everything going your way?"

His words were harsh, but his face held a sincerity that ate at her doubt. Maybe he had something here. She thought she was happy, but was she really? Didn't worrying about everything and falling to pieces when things went wrong deny the very thought of happiness? She'd give this some thought.

Later.

When she wasn't concerned with finding Fuzzy's killer...

"I hear what you're saying—and I'll think about it—but I'm not ready to jump on your religion bandwagon." She glanced at the barn. "Right now we need to call Russ."

Ryan's eyes filled with disappointment. She hated causing this reaction, but she couldn't flip on a religious switch just because he wanted her to believe the same thing he did. After all, she'd said she'd think about it. What more could he expect?

"Do you have Russ's cell number?"

"Yeah. I'll call him." Ryan breathed deep and exhaled, likely releasing his frustration with her. "Seems odd that Russ missed the wallet when collecting evidence."

Indeed, how could he have missed something so obvious? Maybe he wasn't such a good cop after all. Or maybe when Russ conducted the search, the wallet wasn't there.

She let her gaze rove the area in hopes of finding

answers. Bandit lunged at the wallet as if it belonged to him.

That's it!

Her heart thumped against her chest. "Russ didn't miss it—it was Bandit. He knew all the time but couldn't tell us."

Bandit thought she was talking to him and bounded to his feet, dancing with excitement. He jumped and yipped with glee. His plastic cone slammed into Mia's legs and he bounded back.

"I'm a little lost here." Ryan quieted Bandit.

"Don't you see? This is what Bandit stole from the office last night. He picked up Fuzzy's scent when he discovered his body, then he found the same scent in the office, but he couldn't get to the wallet because it was locked up in Verna's file cabinet."

Verna was the murderer.

The pain in Mia's face knotted Ryan's stomach. He'd do anything to take away her hurt. He'd already had a battle in convincing her to leave the barn and come with him to the lodge to wait for Russ's arrival. She'd wanted to dig through the ruins for additional clues, but they couldn't rut through the crime scene.

At the lodge, Ryan had made her a cup of tea, but the cup sat untouched on the counter in front of her as she leaned on her elbows and stared ahead, lost in thought. Maybe she was thinking about what he'd said about God. If only she'd come to trust Him with her life. She'd still be in pain, but it would be so much more bearable.

Perhaps he should follow up and see if she had any additional questions. "Anything you want to talk about?" he asked in a soft tone so as not to startle her.

She offered a wan smile. "I keep wondering why Fuzzy was up here, and I can't figure out a reason at all."

"Maybe he came to visit the place where his friend was always so happy."

"If it was that simple then why would Verna kill him?"

Ryan didn't like how Mia had jumped to this conclusion and stuck with it, but he understood her reasons. The wallet pointed to Verna's guilt. Still, Ryan thought Verna an unlikely murderer. He was all set to tell Mia as much but he saw the police cruiser pull up outside and jumped to his feet.

"Here comes Russ. Maybe he'll have some insight on all of this." Ryan crossed the room and opened the door.

Russ took the stairs two at a time. With a grunt as a greeting, he charged past Ryan and over to Mia.

She sat upright. "Are you going to arrest Verna for killing Fuzzy?"

His eyes creased in confusion. "Fuzzy?"

"Franklin Springer's nickname is Fuzzy," Ryan explained.

Mia leaned forward. "Are you going to arrest her or not?"

"I'll bring her in for questioning, but I don't like her for the murder. Would take a much larger person than Verna to inflict the trauma that killed Springer."

"So she hired the guy who started the fire to do it." Mia's words shot out, colored with desperation. "She's still guilty of planning the murder."

Russ shrugged. "We'll see. There're a lot of loose ends that need investigating before I'm ready to charge her."

Mia's mouth dropped open. "Fuzzy's wallet was in her file cabinet. What more do you need?"

"As much as you want to think you've solved this case, I have no evidence to prove Bandit found the wallet in the file cabinet."

"But we s—"

"No buts, Mia. Charging someone with murder requires real evidence. And we don't have it. Besides, other things don't add up. Like the break-in." He crossed his arms. "Why would Verna hire someone to steal files she could dispose of on her own? And if she did have the wallet in her file cabinet, would she want it exposed in a break-in?"

"Russ is right, Mia. It doesn't make sense." Ryan settled on to the stool next to her and laid a hand on her shoulder. "And Verna doesn't have a good motive to kill Fuzzy, either."

She shot him a look of displeasure, but he had to make her see Russ spoke the truth.

She turned to his brother. "Fuzzy was a private investigator. Maybe he was up here investigating her embezzlement, and she killed him when he discovered it."

"And how would Springer know to investigate her?"

"Maybe Wally asked him to do it before he died."

"He died over three months ago," Ryan said. "Wouldn't Fuzzy have acted sooner, or at least told you about it?"

Mia gave a halfhearted nod. "We keep coming up empty-handed."

"Maybe this will help us move forward." Russ reached into his pocket and pulled out a small scrap of paper. "We found a cell phone outside the office last night. It's a prepaid phone so we can't be sure it's even related to the break-in. There's only one text on the phone, which was sent a little more than a week ago to another prepaid phone. Here's the message. Does this make any sense to either of you?"

He slid the paper across the counter to Mia. She pulled it close.

Ryan leaned over to read. *2533 *5. 36605s*

"That's odd." Mia shared a confused look with Ryan.

Ryan chuckled. "Is this some kind of new texting slang teens use to baffle their parents?"

Russ flashed an irritated glare. "More like a code of some sort, but we haven't been able to crack it." He fixed his eyes on Mia. "I want to go through Pinetree's office again. You can agree to the search, or I can get a warrant."

"You have my permission to do whatever you need to do." She held up the paper. "Can I keep this? In case I can figure it out."

"Knock yourself out." Russ tipped his head at the counter. "But it'd be more helpful if you worked on retrieving a picture from that camera."

Ryan had forgotten all about Chuck's camera sitting where Mia placed it last night.

She nodded. "I'll get it to Chuck when you leave."

Russ headed to the door and paused. "Where can I find you this afternoon if I need you?"

Ryan glanced at the clock. "We have sessions with the students all afternoon."

"Keep your cells on," Russ said, his voice drifting off as he exited.

Ryan listened to the clomping of Russ's feet fading away in the distance. "I guess this is more complicated than we thought."

Mia fiddled with the scrap of paper. "Part of me says the case is solved, and Russ just has to find what he needs to arrest Verna. The other part of me can't believe she's actually responsible for killing Fuzzy."

"Is it easier to believe your father did it?"

Mia sighed. "No. I now know he didn't do this. I accused him for nothing." Her voice broke. "And like David said, I put a rift between us that I'll never repair." She looked up, and her eyes telegraphed an ache that ripped at Ryan's heart.

He couldn't handle seeing her suffer without being able to help. He had to do something…even if it was as simple as holding her.

"It'll be all right," he whispered as he pulled her into an embrace. "I'm with you, and we can face whatever happens together."

Instead of bursting into tears, or even pushing him away, she relaxed and rested her head on his shoulder as if she really believed he would stay by her side through all of this. Her heart said she trusted him. A huge leap from just a few days ago.

He tightened his hold, felt the taut muscles in his shoulders relax as her soft breath whispered over his neck. A nearly overpowering urge to move her away and seek her lips in a kiss came over him.

Not a kiss like the quick peck last night, but a long, heartfelt kiss that conveyed the feelings tumbling inside of him. One like they'd shared years ago when a future together was certain.

Now that the case was winding down, and she would once again be safe, could he hope there might be a future for them?

Or was he getting ahead of himself?

After all, the killer hadn't been apprehended. And

once he was, what then? She could die in a car accident like her mother. Or in so many other ways.

How was he ever going to let go of his fear of giving his heart to a woman and then losing her? More importantly was he ever willing to do what it took to move forward in the face of such high stakes?

EIGHTEEN

Students, dressed in their matching uniforms, sat on the logs and boulders surrounding a smoldering fire with a cast-iron pot centered over the coals. Each tired face frustrated and overwhelmed was like peering into a mirror. The discovery of Fuzzy's identity had left Mia spinning. So had Ryan's comments about God.

Flashes of attending church as a child popped into her mind. The preacher standing on a raised platform declared helping others took focus off your troubles. He spoke the truth. Her counseling practice confirmed that. She would try anything right now to avoid facing the pain of another loss. She was even willing to consider God might be the answer.

What could it hurt to turn to God? As Ryan said, her life wasn't going so well on her own. Maybe she *should* ask God to help her. Maybe He would listen to her.

Maybe later.

When she'd had more time to think it through. Now she'd work on the helping others thing.

She clutched Chuck's camera and searched the group to locate him. She found him on the other side of the snapping fire with his face pressed against a video camera. Nikki stood next to him smiling like an adoring groupie.

Waving wayward smoke from her face, Mia approached him. "I've got bad news for you."

Chuck looked up from the camera. "Ah, man, my baby. She's pretty bad off, isn't she?"

Mia explained what happened. "I'm really sorry, Chuck."

He took the camera and turned it over. "I think I can get the memory card out. Then you might have a picture or two of the jerk who did this."

"I would really appreciate that." Mia nodded at him. "How soon can you get to it?"

"Should have time tonight," he said.

"That would be great."

Chuck turned to Nikki. "Hey. kid. Take this to the editing trailer, will ya?"

Nikki, with hero worship in her eyes, took the camera from Chuck before strolling away.

"And come right back," Chuck yelled after her. "Gotta love the enthusiasm of the little newbie."

"Thanks again, Chuck." Mia smiled her gratitude as he moved back behind the camera and Eddie caught her attention.

Hesitantly, he got up, checked to see if anyone was watching and then sauntered to Chuck in a walk filled with bravado. "Hey, man. Can I look at your camera again?"

Chuck cast furtive glances around. "I told you before—I'm not supposed to do this."

Eddie glowered at Chuck, the strength of his expression giving Mia a moment of discomfort.

"Fine," Chuck said. "I'll give you a few minutes, but this is the last time. Understood?"

Eddie nodded and went straight to the camera. His sullen mouth parted, the corners of his lips quivering. Color had come to his cheeks, and he radiated happiness. He touched the camera with reverence. As he held it, a soft smile of contentment settled into place. He jabbered about lenses, F-stops, filters and lighting. His knowledge of photography techniques spoke to extensive experience.

This made her miss the days Uncle Wally spent teaching her how to use a 35mm camera and how to develop pictures in the darkroom. Those were good days.

Wait! This was it! The connection she needed. Her way to get Eddie to open up and at the same time discover the burglar's identity. Now all she had to do was find Ryan and convince him to implement her unorthodox idea.

Ryan peered across the opening and studied an animated Mia. He should be concentrating on what Ian was saying to the trio he was conversing with but despite the fear that kept raising it's ugly head, he couldn't help but stare at the radiant expression on her face. He didn't know what or who put her in such a good mood but he wished it had been him. Wished she would beam at him the same way. Wished they could figure out who was threatening her so he could let go of his fear and explore feelings that continued to surge through him at the mere sight of her.

She put a hand over her eyes to block the sun and scanned the crowd. She spotted him and motioned for him to join her. This was all the encouragement he needed to leave his group and cross over to her.

When he reached her, she turned him around by his elbow and held him facing Eddie.

"Look at Eddie's face," she said, her voice as exuberant as her expression. "In our session yesterday I couldn't get him to open up at all. But this could be the connection I need."

Ryan studied Eddie and Chuck. "Chuck shouldn't be engaging the students in conversation."

"Ignore that for a minute." She tightened her grip on Ryan's arm. "Chuck said he thought he could get the memory card out of his camera tonight. If you'd let Eddie help work on the camera, I could hang out with them and see what develops."

Ryan smiled. "No pun intended there."

She laughed. "I could broach the subject of cameras and maybe when he sees we have shared interests he'll open up to me. We could take some pictures together, and I can see if Uncle Wally's darkroom equipment is still around here somewhere."

"Okay, okay, slow down." He faced her and rested his hands on her shoulders. "This sounds like a great idea but first we need Chuck to buy into it."

"Do you want to talk to him or should I?"

"I think it'd be best if I did it. Your enthusiasm might scare him off."

"So when can you do it?"

"After our trust exercises this afternoon." He glanced at his watch. "We're on schedule so we should be done about the same time your sessions end."

"And you'll come find me to tell me what he says?"

Was she kidding him? He'd take any excuse to be with her. "Why don't we meet for coffee after we're done?"

With hands still on her shoulders, he drew her closer then let his fingers run down her arms to her hands. "We can catch up on a lot of things." He let his eyes lock on to hers and hoped he transmitted the emotions shooting through his heart.

Her face turned crimson, and she glanced around the group as if nervous about others seeing them. "I guess I better get up to the rec center."

"I'll see you later." He let his tone fill with promise of something special to come when they met again. A promise he hoped he could fulfill.

Following her last session, Mia headed straight to the lodge to make coffee for her upcoming meeting with Ryan. After the emotion-filled look he gave her at the fire pit, she could hardly concentrate on her afternoon sessions. She had to admit she liked the way he'd locked eyes with her and sent her emotions churning in a way she hadn't experienced since the two of them had been together. Sure, she'd dated other men over the years and they'd connected, but not with the same intensity as she'd just experienced with Ryan.

The doorbell chimed, and she jumped. Maybe he'd finished early. She rushed to the door. A quick look through the peephole deflated her excitement. She ran a hand over her hair and took several deep breaths to settle her nervous excitement.

"Hey, you two," she said to Reid and Jessie, inserting as much enthusiasm into her words as possible so as to not let them know she'd hoped to see Ryan.

Reid offered an apologetic smile. "Jessie was wondering if she could spend some time with Bandit."

"Sure," Mia said, stepping back. "I just made coffee. Would you like a cup, Reid?"

"Sounds good to me." Reid smiled his thanks and the pair entered the lodge.

"Bandit," Jessie called with excitement.

He sat up with a confused look.

Jessie studied him with scrunched eyes then looked at Mia. "Why's he pretending to be a lamp?"

Mia smiled at the child's take on his cone and explained the purpose for it. She went to the kitchen to get the coffee. "He was supposed to be taking it easy, but he stayed out all night long. So if you want to play with him, you'll need to keep it kind of calm."

"Aw, no fair. I wanted to be a lamp with him."

Mia laughed. "Lamps don't do much moving around."

"That sounds like being in school." Jessie's lower lip protruded.

"So how come you have the day off?" Mia asked as Jessie came into the kitchen.

"Teacher conference day. Daddy says my teacher told him I was a peach, but I don't know what that means. Daddy says it means I'm a good girl." She gazed up at Mia with beaming eyes.

"That you are, kiddo." Mia turned to Reid and handed him a mug.

"Thanks." He blew on the cup and sat on a counter stool.

"How about a cup of hot chocolate?" Mia asked Jessie and leaned on the countertop next to Reid.

Shaking her head, she pointed ahead. "I wanna play on your computer."

Reid slid forward. "I'm sure Mia doesn't have any games for you to play."

"Nuh-huh. If she can get the Internet, I can play Barbie." Her eyes pleaded. "You have the Internet? Daddy helps me at home, but he probably doesn't know how to on this kind of computer."

Mia set the sleeping laptop in front of Jessie and

she poised her tiny fingers over the keyboard in anticipation.

"It's not much different than a big computer. It's just all packed into one little box." Mia pointed at the touch pad. "Here's the mouse." She slipped her finger along the pad and the computer woke up.

A man's picture filled the screen. Bald-headed, with large dark eyes, he resembled a mean Mr. Clean.

Jessie jerked her face away. "No. Turn it off."

"I don't know where this came from." Mia looked at the name of the file. *Gladys's Suspects*. "It's okay, kiddo. Gladys loaded these pictures last night. He might look mean, but he's just a guy who bought something at the gas station."

"Nah-uh!" Jessie started crying and she tried to push the computer away, but the rubber pads on the bottom held it firmly in place. She pounded on the keys as if she hit the right one it would kill the machine.

"Jessie." Reid stood and grabbed her hands. "That's no way to treat Mia's computer."

"That's the man," she whispered. She closed her eyes and sobbed harder.

"Jessie, what is it?" Mia asked with an urgent voice.

Eyes still closed, Jessie pointed at the computer.

"He did it." Her voice broke on a sob. "He's the man who started the fire."

NINETEEN

Even after Jessie departed with Reid, her fear saturated Mia like a sponge filled with water. Now Lincoln Pope's taunting grin from a mouth surrounded with coarse stubble ramped up her concern. His eyes glinted like hard steel, razor-sharp and deadly. He'd hurt little Jessie not once, but twice now. Mia wanted to punch her computer screen to erase the snarling man's picture, but how would that help?

She pressed the Internet button on her laptop and waited for the slower dial-up service to open the home page. She typed Lincoln Pope in the search box and sat back to stretch a kink from her neck.

"Mia, did you hear me?" Russ asked from the other side of the island where he and Ryan had been discussing this new development.

She looked up. "Sorry, I was running a search on Pope."

"I need to get back to the office." Russ pulled a business card from his uniform shirt. "Here's my e-mail address. Send that picture to me. Sooner rather than later."

"Don't worry," Mia said. "I'll send it right now."

Russ left and she turned back to the computer. "What on earth?"

"What is it?" Ryan asked.

She pointed at the screen where *35nc63n *6*e* appeared in the search box. "I typed *Lincoln Pope* in the search engine and this is what came up."

"That's odd. Maybe you were distracted and mistyped."

"I'll do it again." She studied the keyboard and punched the right keys for Lincoln Pope.

"Same thing," Ryan said.

She typed other words. "Left hand keys work fine. Right is screwed up."

Ryan shook his head. "Looks like you're typing in Morse code."

"Morse code?" She peered at the keyboard, then at the text message on the counter. She shot to her feet and ran to the door.

"Russ," she shouted, halting him as he climbed into his car. "Come back. I know who killed Fuzzy."

Ryan studied the keyboard to see if he could figure out what Mia had discovered. Since his comment about Morse code sparked a fire in her, it had to have something to do with a code, but what?

"C'mon," Mia said to Russ and rushed to the computer while he followed. "You're probably familiar with Num Lock on a full-sized keyboard, right?"

Russ rolled his eyes. "When it's pushed, the

numbers on the side of the keyboard work. If not they don't."

"It's not the same on a laptop if it doesn't have a number pad." She pointed at the right side of the keyboard. "See how these letters have numbers on the front of the keys. If you look at the arrangement it looks just like the number pad on a full-sized keyboard. When Num Lock is activated on a laptop these keys turn into numbers, not letters."

"So." Russ's tone was bored.

"When Jessie spotted Pope's picture and she tried to push the computer away, the rubber feet kept it from moving. So she pounded on the keys in frustration, and she accidently turned on Num Lock." Mia slid the paper with the text message toward Russ. "If you compare this to the keyboard with Num Lock turned on, 2533 *5. 36605s, spells Kill PI. Loomis."

Russ straightened up. "Kurt Loomis?"

"Loomis?" Ryan asked, catching Mia's excitement. "Why would Loomis tell Pope to kill Fuzzy?"

Russ offered one of his rare smiles. "A good question. One I intend to ask him when I bring him in for questioning."

"So this is enough to arrest him?" Mia asked.

"Arrest? No. Interrogate? Definitely." Russ jogged to the door. "I'll let you know what we find out."

"You are brilliant." Ryan swept Mia off the stool and swung her around. She giggled like a schoolgirl and wrapped her arms around his shoulders

This was the Mia he remembered. Full of life and excited over new discoveries. The Mia, if he were totally honest, who had found a way to open his heart again.

He set her down, and she peered up at him. He expected to see clear eyes filled with joy, instead a spark of unease tainted the deep green shade. "What's wrong?"

"We may have figured some of this out, but we still don't know where Pope is—and it looks like he's the killer."

Renewed fear over her safety sent Ryan's interest ebbing away like the ocean surf heading out to sea. He sucked in air and cleared his head. "Guess you better send that picture to Russ."

She returned to the computer and clicked F11. "That should turn off Num Lock."

"How'd you know about that anyway?"

"I accidently turned it on one day and had to get a computer tech to tell me what was wrong." She surfed to her e-mail provider, opened a new message and typed a short note then attached the picture file. She looked up. "In all the excitement, I forgot to ask if you had time to talk to Chuck about working with Eddie tonight."

"I did. He's cool with it."

Mia nodded. "Good. If we can produce a picture of Pope from the camera, it'll be one more piece of evidence to put him behind bars." She started typing again. "I'm gonna mention that in this e-mail, too, so Russ knows about it."

Ryan stood back and watched Mia's fingers fly over the keyboard. Her tongue peeked out the side of her mouth as she paid full attention to her work. Hopefully, this message would result in the arrest of Pope, and she would once again be safe.

She hit Send, then peered up at him with a spectacular smile that warmed his heart. His pulse quickened. He wanted to let go of his fear of losing her. Wanted to sweep her into his arms. Wanted to tell her what she meant to him.

Help me let go of this fear, Lord.

The e-mail program finished and the computer screen cleared, bringing Pope's hard face back into view. Mia was far from safe until this man was captured.

Ryan's heart constricted with pain. He couldn't let go…not yet.

Mia sat next to Ryan in the John Deere as they drove toward the documentary crew's equipment trailer where she would meet with Eddie. Throughout the day, she'd managed to tamp down her fear of Pope, and as they drove toward the blazing orange ball of a setting sun, a peaceful feeling about being with Ryan settled over her. She would actually miss him when he left her at the trailer for a staff meeting in the rec center.

Somehow, she'd let him get close. Too close and

she had no idea how she was going to deal with that. Didn't know if she wanted to fight the emotion or give in. Sure he'd been controlling, but through his domineering ways she could see his reasoning. Feel his caring. Understand his motives.

She glanced at him as he parked the cart near the trailer. His strong profile gave her confidence. His presence, hope.

Russ's cruiser came barreling down the drive, forcing Ryan to hit the brakes hard. He shot out a hand to stop Mia from slamming into the dash. She clasped his muscled arm and knew in that instance that he would always act to protect her. She had come to trust him to know what was good for her and when to back off. Still, she had no idea what to do with these emotions.

"Sorry about that," Ryan said as he climbed from the vehicle.

"Not your fault." Mia joined him and waved away the churned up dust as they made their way to the cruiser where Russ had already rolled down his window.

"Loomis sang like an *American Idol* contestant," he said.

"What'd he tell you?" Mia leaned toward the window.

Russ turned the volume down on his squawking radio. "Turns out he has a gambling problem, and he embezzled money from Pinetree a few years ago. Wally found out about it, but instead of prosecuting

Loomis, he gave him a chance to straighten up and repay the money."

Mia smiled as pictures of her trusting uncle flashed in her memory. "Sounds like Wally. He was always more than willing to give people a second chance."

Russ's expression turned skeptical. "Yeah, well I'd never let a guy who stole from me remain in charge of my finances."

"Wally must have thought of that, too," Mia said. "David told me they made some changes in how the books were handled. Maybe that was to keep Loomis from taking more money."

"So if this happened a few years ago, what changed to set Loomis off?" Ryan asked.

"Wally's death. Loomis knew he'd have to prepare reports for the transition in ownership, and his embezzlement would come out. Then he got the bright idea if he scared you away, David would inherit and not ask for any reports. So he hired Pope."

"But how did he get my bracelet?" Mia asked.

"Accidentally, that's how. He'd paid the bills for Pinetree for years so he knew about a large storage unit Wally kept. He was afraid the unit held files with proof of his embezzlement so he broke into it." He shrugged. "Instead, he found items from your house in Atlanta. David told him about how your dad wouldn't let you keep anything so he knew the bracelet would freak you out."

"Wally kept a whole storage unit of our things?

Why didn't he tell me?" A cold wave hit Mia, and she instinctively sought Ryan's gaze for comfort.

He came closer.

"I don't know about that," Russ's voice turned soft. "But at least you now have something to remember your mother by."

He was right—this was a good thing in disguise. She might have a whole shed full of positive things. But why had Wally kept it a secret all of these years? Was he guilty of betraying her...?

No, she wouldn't think that way about him. For some reason he knew she wasn't ready to see them. He was also right when he decided she'd want these memories. She couldn't wait to get her hands on them, but first they needed to connect the remaining dots.

"So how did Fuzzy get mixed up in this?" Mia asked as Ryan wrapped an arm around her. She moved into the warmth.

"Loomis got greedy." Russ's tone was unforgiving. "Confident he'd make you leave, he not only quit paying back the money, but found a way to steal more. What he didn't count on, was Wally had told Fuzzy all about the embezzlement—and Fuzzy wasn't so trusting. He decided to check up on Loomis. Caught him and Loomis ordered Pope to kill him."

"He admitted ordering Pope to kill Fuzzy?" Her tone turned shrill.

Ryan shushed her. "They'll hear you." He tipped his head at the trailer

"Sorry," Mia said.

Russ's face turned deadly serious. "Not only to kill him, but to dispose of the body. Pope must have thought he could take care of the body and start the fire at the same time. He just wasn't smart enough to do it right." Russ lifted a travel cup from a holder and took a long sip.

"What about the office break-in?" Ryan asked. "Was that Pope, too?"

Russ nodded. "Except he wasn't stealing any-thing—he was planting files that pointed at Verna for the embezzlement. Pope put Springer's wallet in the file cabinet a few days earlier, and when he went back to add the files, he staged the break-in so we would find the wallet and the files."

"And we fell for it." Mia felt like a fool. "Now all we have to do is find Pope."

"I have an APB out, but I imagine he's long gone by now. If he hasn't split before today, when he hears we picked up Loomis, he'll figure Loomis will give him up and he'll take off."

Mia looked up at the trailer. "As much as I want him caught, even if he does get away, at least Kurt isn't ordering him to do anything else." She lifted her head up and let a warm smile settle over Ryan. "Now we can get on with life and help these kids."

Ryan returned her smile with a flirtatious grin that kicked her pulse into high gear.

Russ groaned. "Can't you two wait for this mushy stuff until I leave?"

"You waiting for an invitation to go?" Ryan asked, not taking his eyes off Mia.

"Don't let your guard down too much. Pope may still be hanging around." Russ revved the engine.

Ryan stepped back and drew Mia with him. She rested the back of her head against his chest and let out a sigh of contentment. She had no idea what was going on in Ryan's mind, but standing with him felt right. So right she wanted to turn and kiss him.

This reaction stunned her. Had she not only let him get close but had she actually fallen for him again?

"Ready to meet with Eddie?" His breath stirred her hair.

"With all of this stuff behind us, I'm more ready than ever." She reluctantly pulled away.

They walked to the makeshift wooden stairs leading to the door of the editing trailer. The wind pulled a strand of her hair free from her clip and whipped it over her face.

Ryan caught the ends and tucked them behind her ear. "I'll be in the rec center if you need me." He slowly lowered his head.

Mia waited, her breath coming in little pulses against the chilly air. She forgot about Eddie and the murders, closed her eyes and lifted her arms around his neck.

Nothing. She flashed open her eyes.

With a groan, he slid his hands up her arms and pulled them down. He took a step back, and let a finger trail down her cheek. "Eddie's waiting." His tone conveyed his reluctance to leave, so why did he set her aside like this?

She drew in a hearty breath to cool her rushing emotions.

How had she so readily responded to him? She didn't know what she was doing anymore. Was she leading Ryan on, or was she ready to commit to a future with him?

A future that meant she would have to remain in Logan Lake. The love for his job shone on his face every minute he was with the students. She would never ask him to leave his life behind to move to Atlanta. He'd probably agree to go, but he belonged here.

She had to be careful to keep things less intense when she saw him later. At least until she figured out what she wanted.

Her cell rang and she dug it out of her jeans pocket. A local number. Maybe David. Good. She longed to tell him she'd been wrong about their father and admit how much she wanted to mend fences with him…

"Hello."

"I just read the newspaper. The front page is devoted to all the things that have happened since you came back. I knew something like this would happen." Her father's stern tone shot through the phone, dashing her hopes for reconciliation. He was clearly embarrassed over the publicity, and felt a need to run damage control. He always had to be in control.

Like her. Keep things within her scope of containment then she didn't get hurt. But that wasn't true. Look at her now. She'd worked so diligently to take back her life, but bad things kept coming. She couldn't control anything. Finding the body proved beyond doubt that she couldn't stop life from unfolding. Her efforts had been futile. So had his. No matter his iron will, her mother died, and Mia rebelled.

Oh, my gosh.

She fell back against the railing. She'd been a thorn in his side, making it harder on him. Pushing, testing, trying. Like rough sandpaper, scraping away. Much the same way Ryan had acted with her.

True, her father had been the mature one in the relationship and should have behaved differently, but she was supposedly mature now, too, and look at how she was handling things. Making a real mess is what she was doing. On all fronts. She had to stop. Find another way or she'd end up bitter and angry like her father.

Time to make a change. Extend the verbal hand of compromise. "I'm sorry if this embarrassed you."

"Embarrassed?" His audible frustration that sent her running in the past, swept over her like a tidal wave. "I wasn't embarrassed. I just wanted to see if you were okay."

"You did?" Her tone was like a little child, uncertain and begging for confirmation from the man who was supposed to love her.

Silence flooded over the phone, uncomfortable and awkward. She waited with held breath for him finally to make the effort to be her father.

She heard him rummaging around and then he cleared his throat. "I have an emergency page. I have to go."

She turned toward the door like a wooden soldier. She'd tried to open her heart and let him in but what did she get? The same treatment. Maybe she was so unlovable she was destined to be alone. Maybe God really did want it that way and if Ryan was right about how God operated, He would have His way and she had no say in the matter.

TWENTY

Mia may have struck out again with her father and may even end up alone in life, but Eddie didn't have to suffer the same outcome. She would make certain of that. She entered the trailer. Chuck and Eddie leaned over a table at the far end of the space. Her life was far from what she hoped it might be, but it cheered her to see Eddie bonding with someone. Even if they couldn't retrieve a photo from the camera, she'd accomplished the best goal of all. Getting Eddie involved in something with the hope that he might finally want to talk about his problems and work toward healing.

Chuck looked up. "Hey, Mia."

She waved, and Eddie's head popped up. When they made eye contact, he groaned and returned his attention to their work. She was intruding. But she wouldn't leave. She sat at a table by the door to wait for a better time to join in.

Watching their profiles, she enjoyed the contrast of coloring. Eddie's hair, blond and long, Chuck's dark and buzzed. Seated on opposite sides of a workbench, their heads pressed together over the camera. Eddie held the camera body and Chuck a small tool.

"Now, where were we?" Chuck asked.

Eddie shot a quick glance at her. "Not with her here."

"No sweat," Chuck said. "You don't have to talk about it anymore if you don't want to."

"I just don't need the stuff *she* always gives me about opening up and talking about my *feelings*."

"Like I said. No need."

"Nah, man. I mean, I like talking to you. You're cool." Eddie slipped needle-nose pliers around something Chuck held out. "It's just, you know, all these counselors harassing me gets to be too much."

Chuck looked up. "Maybe you should listen to them. Tell them the same things you told me."

"Why?" Eddie's voice held challenge.

"Because they're trained to help you. I'm just a guy who likes cameras and they thought working with me would help you feel more comfortable around them."

Eddie set his tool on the bench and stared at Chuck until he looked up. "So you're saying you're only working with me because they made you do it?"

Chuck glanced at Mia, his eyes wary.

"Don't look at her. This is between you and me."

Chuck pulled his hefty body upright and ran a hand around the back of his neck. "Look, man. It doesn't matter. You got the chance to work on the camera instead of doin' those sissy group things. Just let it go at that."

Eddie shoved his stool back so hard it toppled and hit the floor. "No way. You tell me why you're doing this, or I'm outta here. Right now. For good."

Chuck planted his palms on the bench. "Fine. I wanted to work on the camera alone, but Ryan convinced me to let you help. All right?"

Eddie looked around, his eyes wild and angry. He let them linger on Mia, burning a hole in her.

She met his gaze, but didn't know what to say. He was really freaked out. Not a surprising reaction for Eddie, whose emotions simmered just beneath the surface waiting to erupt with little provocation. And not surprising when he'd expressed frustration over people not having pure motives in helping him.

"Look, man," Chuck said, drawing Eddie's attention. "No biggie. Let's get back to work."

"Dude, I knew she would sell me out. But you…I trusted you." Eddie's last few words came out in a scream as he lunged at Chuck, fists flying.

She rushed at them. "Eddie—please. I know you're hurt but this won't help."

He spun on her. His face was contorted with rage like she'd never seen. She took a step back. Chuck got up and reached for Eddie. The teen charged at Chuck, shoving him to the side. He fell hard. Eddie dropped on top and pummeled Chuck.

"Mia, get some help," Chuck shouted. "I don't wanna hurt him."

Eddie might calm down or this might escalate, but she couldn't take the chance on it intensifying. If he pushed this, Chuck had to defend himself, and both of them could get hurt.

Ryan could help. She rushed out the door and ran for the rec center.

Feet pounding, heart racing, she charged into the room and up to Ryan who sat behind a long table, head bent over a project.

"We need you at the trailer." She breathed deep.

"Be with you in a sec. Almost done here," he said.

She didn't want the others in the room to know what was going on but she needed to get Ryan to move quickly. "Now! It's Eddie!"

Ryan's head flew up, and he quickly got to his feet. He jogged across the floor, and she fell into step beside him.

"What's going on?" he asked with concern.

"Chuck and Eddie got into it, and Eddie's raging mad. He attacked Chuck."

Ryan mumbled something under his breath that Mia couldn't make out, and he upped his pace. In far better shape and without any injuries, he took off, reached the trailer and disappeared inside.

Her side ached from the round trip. She stopped to catch her breath.

All was quiet. Good. Maybe they had stopped fighting. She listened. Heard footfalls.

Ryan came to the door.

"You got your cell?" His eyes were strained, and his mouth flattened in a tight line.

She nodded, her stomach starting to sink.

"Call 911."

She stepped closer to the door. "What happened?"

Ryan stared into the night. "It's Chuck. He's dead."

Ryan wanted nothing more than to get away from the lights of the police cars screaming through the night. Not to mention the stunned and terrified expression lodged in Mia's eyes.

She'd called 911 and then drew into herself and had barely said a word. He'd tried to comfort her, but she'd shaken off his arm and snapped at him. He knew she was blaming herself for Chuck's death, and wasn't herself right now, but her rebuff hurt.

However, he had a more pressing matter to deal with right now.

Sighing with resignation, he braced for more upheaval as he watched Russ storm toward them snapping off latex gloves as he walked. His face was fixed in a deep scowl and he had his sights set on Mia.

She wrapped her arms around her waist and backed up as if trying to run away before he arrived. Ryan wanted to intervene, but he had to let Russ do his job.

He stopped in front of Mia. "You're sure the camera was here when you left?"

"Positive," Mia said. "They were working on it before the fight broke out."

He stuffed the gloves into his back pocket. "Well, it's gone now. Most logical explanation is that the kid hit Kowalski with the camera then took off with the murder weapon."

"No." Mia shook her head side to side. "Eddie's not a killer. A mixed-up kid who got angry, but not a killer."

"For what it's worth," Ryan said, offering Mia a nod of acknowledgment, "I agree with Mia. Since Eddie's parents died, he values life too much to kill someone."

Russ scrunched his eyes as if mulling it over. "You could be right, but he split, casting suspicion his way."

Ryan held up a hand. "Not so fast, bro. Eddie most likely ran because he thought we'd send him back to juvie after going off on Chuck."

"Possible. The kid remains my number-one suspect, but I'll look at other possibilities, too."

Mia stepped closer and clutched Russ's jacket sleeve. "What other possibilities?"

"For one, it might have been Pope coming back to get the camera because his picture is on it."

"How would he know who had the camera?" Ryan asked.

"I don't know. Maybe he's kept a better watch on things around here than we thought."

Mia shuddered, and Ryan wanted to pull her close,

but the look in her eyes forbid him from doing so. "Say it *was* Pope. He took the camera. So why kill Chuck?"

"Simple. He's not sure if Kowalski saw the picture of him and can ID him so he has to kill him."

"Yes, that makes sense." Mia's tone bordered on hysterical. "You should go after Pope and leave Eddie alone."

"Can't do that, Mia. Until I have proof Pope is our guy, Eddie Cramer is wanted for the murder of Kowalski." Russ pulled in a deep breath. "You both can go. I'll call if I need anything else."

"Go? Where can I go to get away from this mess?" Mia burst into tears.

With a sympathetic look for Ryan, Russ fled back to the trailer.

She lowered her head. "This is all my fault. If I didn't get the two of them together, Chuck would be alive."

"Shh. This isn't your fault at all." Ryan ignored her warning look and wrapped his arm around her shoulders. "You know as well as I do Eddie didn't kill Chuck. If Pope wanted to find Chuck, he'd have found him no matter where he was."

"But I took the pictures of Pope. And I gave the camera back to Chuck." Her voice fell off into a silence that hung eerily in the heavy night air.

He held her tightly against his chest as her body shook. Her sobs pulled at his heart. He had to find a way to help her through this. He'd hold her until she got the initial shock out of her system, then they could talk and he'd do his best to help her see she was not to blame. He lifted his head and prayed for the miracle it would take to help Mia recover from this nightmare.

Mia stood to the side and watched the medical examiner drive off with Chuck's body. Ryan had mothered her, urging her to leave the scene and get some rest, but she didn't want to go in case word about Eddie came in. She couldn't handle the tension radiating around them, and she'd snapped, shooing Ryan away. His eyes had creased with the pain of her snub, and she instantly wanted to take it back, but let him go anyway. In this mood, she was poison to herself. She didn't want to infect him with it, too.

Every few minutes her eyes drifted toward him. Right now, he chatted with his crew, offering them the comfort she'd refused. He'd chosen his profession well. The staff members gazed at him with respect and appreciation for his compassion. He would make a fine life companion, but the earlier call with her father showed her she could never let go of her past. And if her past continued to haunt her, she'd never fully trust Ryan.

He caught her gaze, and excused himself from the group.

"Have you decided how I can help?" His voice was gentle, caring. Inviting her to let him help.

She couldn't give him the chance. "This is my

problem. I caused it, so I need to fix it." Her tone was harsher than needed, but if she let him have any opening, he would be sucked into her world. A world that could only cause him more pain.

He crossed his arms. "Just like that, huh? I thought we'd gotten beyond our past. Now, a little trouble comes and you shove me out of your life."

She hated hurting him but that couldn't be helped. "I'm sorry but I've pretty much been on my own for ten years, and I like it that way." She sounded so convincing, she almost believed it herself.

"Right, like I buy that." He rested on a fence rail. "If you'd talk to me about how you feel, it could only get better."

Ohh, feelings.

Her imitation of Eddie's sarcasm in their counseling session made the tears prick her eyes again. She turned and walked to the end of the fence so Ryan wouldn't see her cry. He'd only push harder if he did.

She looked at the stars and the vast night sky, her tears sliding down her cheeks. She was just like Eddie. Ryan could no more help her than she could help Eddie, unless they chose to let someone into their closed-off world.

Ryan's soft footfalls coming closer sent her into panic mode. She had to either give in to him completely—or send him packing.

She spun and did what she did best. "I need to

be alone. I've been feeling vulnerable since I got to town, but I'm better now."

He stared at her, long and hard, until she looked to the side. "It's a funny thing, Mia. When I see someone crying, I don't think the person is okay."

She swiped her sleeve across her face. "Well, I am. Please, just go."

Slowly he turned and took a few steps where he paused and looked back at her. "This time, I'm gone for good. Unless you ask me to come back."

Their eyes locked. "I won't ask," she said and returned her gaze to the sky as if it could help her.

Maybe she was searching for God up there. Ryan said God was supposed to fix everything. Why would He fix this when He allowed it? The worst thing she could imagine had come to pass and it was her fault. She might as well have killed Chuck herself for as bad as she was feeling.

Ryan drew a huge breath and let it out slowly as he glanced at Mia standing near the trailer. He couldn't believe she just sent him packing when he wanted to help her so badly.

Had he misread her actions today? Did she really want to be alone for the rest of her life, or did she just not want to be with him? And he never got a chance to help her see God was still here. He hadn't deserted her no matter their relationship.

A cue Ryan needed to follow right now. God hadn't given up on her so neither could he. She may have put distance between them, but he would do his best to be sure she stayed safe, giving him another chance to help her see her need for God. While she cooled off, he'd talk with Russ about the safety of his staff and students.

Ryan crossed over to Russ whose cell phone jangled from his belt holder. He lifted the phone to his ear.

"What's up, Reid?" he asked as he took his hat off and clapped it against his knee. His face contorted, and he locked gazes with Ryan. "What do you mean she's missing?"

Ryan took a step closer.

"I'm on my way." Russ's face paled to an eerie white.

Ryan recognized that haunted look from Russ's last days in Portland when a child was murdered and he blamed himself for the death. Something beyond horrible had happened.

Dear Lord, what now?

Ryan was nearly afraid to ask, but he had to know. "Russ, what is it?"

"That was Reid." His voice caught. "Jessie's missing."

Mia couldn't have heard Russ right. He said Jessie was missing, but what exactly did he mean by that? She raced toward him. "Missing how?"

The fear in the strong lawman's eyes upped her anxiety.

He shoved his phone into the clip. "Reid put her to bed about an hour ago. He just checked on her, and she's gone. I think Pope found out she saw him in the barn, and he's tying up loose ends."

"Pope? But how could he know?"

Russ shook his head. "I don't know, and I don't have time to discuss it." He pivoted like a precision soldier and faced Ryan. "If Pope is still in the area, I need you to get your staff and the kids into the rec center and lock the door. Mia, you go with them. I'll post one of my men to make sure you're all safe." He returned to his men and barked urgent orders.

Mia stood woodenly in place. How could this be? Little Jessie in the hands of a killer all because Kurt Loomis embezzled money?

She should go to the rec center like Russ said, but she couldn't. This whole tragedy was brought on because Loomis wanted her gone. If she stayed with the students and staff, she might bring danger to their doorstep. She couldn't do that. And if Pope had Jessie, Mia had to try to find them. To free Jessie.

She turned and rushed to the John Deere, ignoring Ryan's calls.

Hard to believe it had only been two hours since he'd sat next to her as they'd driven to this end of the property.

Two hours.

One death and one kidnapping ago.

What would the next hour bring, and could she possibly survive it?

TWENTY ONE

Too bad the driveway was unpaved or Mia would've burned rubber as she floored the gas in her rental car. She had to find Jessie before Pope did something horrific to the sweet young girl. But where had he taken her? He wasn't from around here. Still, he'd been living somewhere close. Mia's best chance to find her was to interrogate the manager of the only hotel in town.

Back tires skidded, and she eased her foot up to safely make her way to the main road. She was about to turn on to the highway when her cell chimed. Caller ID didn't display a name, but she answered in case it was an update on Eddie or Jessie.

"Mia, it's Sydney."

Mia sighed out her disappointment. Nothing to do with Jessie. Sydney was probably calling to gossip about Kurt.

"What's up, Sydney?" Mia asked with little patience.

"Is the documentary crew still filming over there?"

"Nothing was scheduled tonight, why?"

Sydney exhaled audibly through the phone. "Nikki got a call an hour or so ago. Said they wanted her to help with the filming. But it's getting late and she's still out. I'm starting to freak."

Clearly, Nikki had lied; she wasn't at Pinetree.

"There's no filming going on, Sydney. Do you know who called Nikki?"

"She was acting all secretive. So maybe she just snuck out to meet a boy again. I'm really gonna let her have it when she gets home."

"Well, call me when she does." Mia disconnected and sighed. The last thing she needed was to worry about a missing teen, too. She turned on the signal, but sat at the end of the driveway.

What if Nikki was connected to this somehow?

Mia thought back to Nikki's behavior with the crew and students. She'd flirted with all the boys as Sydney had feared, but now that Mia thought about it, Nikki watched Eddie a lot. Maybe Eddie called her. But his cell had been confiscated. Still, if Eddie was on the run, a fellow teen and an impressionable girl would be a likely person to call. She knew the area and could make sure he had a safe place to hide.

Mia rang Sydney back. "Does your uncle still have that place on the lake?"

"Yeah, why?"

"Call 911 and tell them you think Nikki took Eddie there."

"What? Eddie who?"

"No time to explain...just do it. Russ's office will understand."

Mia clicked off and dropped her cell into her coat pocket. She ignored the clicking blinker and turned south. The cabin was less than two miles away. In high school she used to party with Sydney's cousin and his friends at the cabin. It was so secluded no one ever caught them. A perfect place for Nikki to hide Eddie.

She took the sharp curves like a race-car driver until she reached the highway, and headed east. She probably should have called Russ, but he needed to find Jessie and bringing Eddie in shouldn't be a big deal. Though she couldn't handle him earlier, she was sure when she explained what happened and that Pope could come after Eddie next, he'd be willing to go with her to the police station.

At the cabin driveway, Mia slowed and turned right. She maneuvered the car as far down the rutted drive as she could without risking Eddie seeing her headlights.

Without a flashlight, her trip down the steep incline was slow. One car was parked in the drive. She didn't know what kind of car Nikki drove but this was a small car, a good choice for a teenager.

Keeping low, Mia made her way to the vehicle and looked inside. A girl's garter, pink fuzzy dice, and a lipstick on a string hung on the rearview mirror. Nikki's car for sure.

Mia squatted and watched the cabin for signs of life.

There. A flash inside.

They were smart enough not to turn on any lamps and they moved around by flashlight. She approached the back door with caution. Slowly, she turned the knob and slipped inside. She could easily get to the front room where she saw the flashlight without turning on a light. She crept along the kitchen cupboards and stepped into the hall.

Soft crying came from the bedroom at the end. A muted conversation drifted from the front room. All of the rooms remained dark.

Indecision crowded in. If she eavesdropped on the conversation, she might learn something that could help her. She stuck with her plan and turned toward the family room.

"Who's gonna believe me?" A male voice sounding like Eddie asked.

"I can vouch for you. I've never been in trouble. They'll believe me." Mia guessed that was Nikki.

"Nah, I can't risk it. If they think I had something to do with this, I'll go away for a long time. You need to take the kid to the cops and tell them what happened."

Kid?

"And what about you? You gonna hoof it all the way back to Portland?"

"I don't know, but I'm not turnin' myself in."

Before either of them decided to make a move it

was time to announce her presence. She spun around the corner and felt along the wall where she knew a switch was located.

Light flooded the room, blinding her. She blinked and counted on Eddie having the same reaction so he didn't jump her or run.

"Mia," Nikki shouted. "I'm so glad you're here."

"What's going on? Who's in the bedroom?"

Nikki's gaze flitted to the doorway. "This isn't what it looks like."

"Shut up, Nikki. Don't tell her anything." Eddie crossed his arms.

"No, you shut up, Eddie. You didn't do anything wrong. Mia will help us."

"Oh, yeah, she's all about helping," he said, sarcasm liberally flowing.

"I asked who's in the bedroom."

"Jessie Morgan."

"What? Jessie!" Mia yelled. "It's Mia. Are you all right?"

Mia heard the door creak open and the slide of small feet on the wood floor of the hallway. Dressed in teddy bear footed pj's, Jessie turned the corner, spotted Mia and raced ahead. Jessie slammed into Mia and wrapped her arms around her waist as if she'd never let go again.

"You okay?" Mia clutched her and bent her head to lay it on Jessie's soft curls.

She nodded. "Eddie saved me."

Mia looked at Eddie. "If ever there was a time for you to talk to me, now's the time."

Nikki nudged him. "Do it. You can trust her."

His gaze raced around the room as if he were looking for any way out other than placing his trust in her. Mia knew the feeling. She'd just been in the same spot with Ryan. She hoped Eddie was smarter than she was and took the best route.

He slapped his palms on his knees, just below the hem of his baggy shorts, and stared at Mia as if daring her to question him. "I was fightin' with Chuck. You saw that. But then when you left, Chuck pinned me down. I got to thinkin' and was worried I would get into trouble and get sent back to juvie. I convinced Chuck to let me up. I went outside and ran around the back of the trailer. I saw this dude sneaking up in the dark. I figured it was one of the guys playing a joke. So I kept goin'. Then I spotted a car and thought about stealin' it or hiding in the back to get out of there. I opened the front door and found a phone on the seat."

He stopped to glance at Nikki who returned his gaze with a nod of encouragement.

Eddie continued. "Nikki gave me her number to use after I got out of this stupid program. So I called her. She said she'd come talk to me. We decided to meet at that place out in the woods where we did the trust exercises. Then I heard this noise in the backseat. Jessie was on the floor. Tied up with tape over her mouth. When she saw me she started crying."

Jessie let go of Mia and ran to Eddie. She wrapped her arms around his neck. "I was scared. But Eddie said he would help me."

Eddie nodded. "So I picked her up and ran into the woods. We waited for Nikki to get there. Then we came here."

"You're a hero, Eddie." Mia's voice rang with conviction.

"You believe me?"

"Of course and so will the police." Mia crossed the room and patted him on the back. Then it dawned on her. He probably didn't have any idea what happened to Chuck. "Did you see the guy who went into the trailer?"

"I saw him come out and drive away. I don't think he knew Jessie was gone when he left."

"Well, he knows now." A crusty male voice came from the hallway as a gun-toting hand shot around the corner. A hand connected to the man she'd come to know as Lincoln Pope.

Ryan left Ian in charge at the rec center and headed for the lodge. He'd been torn between making sure the staff and students were safe and checking on Mia who'd foolishly fled into the night. The students and staff had a deputy. Mia was alone; she needed him.

He reached the lodge and found the door unlocked. Panic blasted into his body.

Had Pope gotten to Mia, too?

God, please, no. Don't let anything happen to Mia.

Eyes wild, searching for anything that might help him find her, his gaze landed on Wally's gun cabinet. He didn't know where she was, but at least he could be armed as he went in search.

The cabinet was locked. He grabbed a bird statue and crashed it into the glass. He chose a revolver Wally had taught all of them to shoot one summer.

Why hadn't Mia thought to take this gun? Maybe she didn't have the chance.

Making sure it held a full clip, he shoved the holstered weapon into his belt then ran outside to the sound of Russ's squad car careening down the driveway. He slammed on his brakes, nearly sideswiping Ryan's truck and causing the squad car to fishtail to a stop.

Russ lowered the window. "Mia found Eddie. They're at Nate Tucker's cabin. I'm headed there now and will call if I hear anything."

"Are you kidding me?" Ryan said. "I'm coming with you." He shot around the front of the car before Russ could take off again. He jerked open the door.

"This is official business." Russ glared at him across the front seat. "You need to wait here."

Ryan slid in. "Then you're gonna have to waste time dragging me out of here. I'm not moving."

Russ upped the intensity of his gaze, but Ryan fired back a more deadly glare.

"Fine." Russ shifted into gear. "I don't have time to waste arguing, but when we get to the cabin, you stay in the car." He flipped on the lights and siren and they headed south on the highway leaving a wailing trail in their wake.

Ryan buckled his seat belt as Russ turned his attention to piloting the car.

At the speed they soon reached, Ryan decided to keep quiet for the ride so Russ could concentrate. They'd only argue about what would happen when they got to the cabin anyway. Not that Ryan had a question in his mind about what he would do. He would be out of the car before Russ could stop him.

As they approached the intersection nearest to the cabin, Russ flipped off the sirens and strobing lights. "Don't want to tell them we're coming."

He slowed and navigated the turn, leaning the car so precariously Ryan had to grab the door handle to keep from sliding into Russ.

The car righted itself in waves. The radio squawked, begging for Russ's already divided attention. Ryan issued a prayer for safety then listened in to see what he could pick up from the initial police speak Russ traded with his dispatcher.

"I have a call to patch through the 911 operator from a Mia Blackburn," the female dispatcher said dispassionately. "She says it's regarding your missing niece."

No need to interpret that. Ryan sat forward and shared a worried look with Russ.

"Russ, are you there?" Mia's shaky voice came through the radio loud and clear.

"Go ahead, Mia."

"I have Jessie at the cabin with me."

"Is she okay?" Russ shouted as if yelling would make the answer what he wanted to hear.

"She's fine. A little scared, but fine."

A scuffling noise and arguing voices came over the phone. Russ slowed the car and stared at Ryan.

"Morgan, this is Lincoln Pope. Since you know all about me, I won't bother introducing myself." Pope ended with a disembodied laugh.

"He has Mia and Jessie," Ryan whispered and clenched his fist to keep from smashing it into the dashboard. "You need to speed up again."

Russ made a slashing motion across his throat and pointed at the cabin's driveway up ahead.

"What do you want, Pope?" Russ asked as he maneuvered the vehicle around another squad car parked at the mouth of the driveway and turned on to the unpaved drive.

"I want to get out of here alive, and you're gonna help me do it."

"Not a chance, Pope," Russ spat back and sent the car down the steep drive.

"You forget. I have your niece here, and I'm not opposed to hurting her." He paused. "Hold that thought." The phone fell silent.

"What he's up to?" Russ brought the car near the house and parked behind the other cars in the driveway.

Ryan scanned the cabin and spotted light seeping out from the blinds. "They're in the family room. Someone's looking through the blinds."

"That you in the driveway?" Pope asked all irritated. "'Cause if it is, I suggest you back on oughta here if you want to help your niece."

"Let's cut to the chase, Pope. What do you want?" Russ demanded.

"Listen up, Morgan. I'll only say this once. I want a clear path to my car. Get all your men off the property and make sure there are no roadblocks. If I see one person or one roadblock, your pretty little niece is history."

"How do I know you won't hurt her anyway?"

"Guess you'll just have to trust me." He laughed again. "Call me back when your men have cleared out. Oh, and Morgan, I'll be watching your car leave so don't try anything funny." The line went dead.

Ryan reached for the door handle. "I'm going in there."

Russ grabbed Ryan's arm. "No way, bro. You don't have a clue what to do in there."

Ryan shook him off. "So what do you suggest? That we sit around and wait for Pope to kill again? One of us has to go in. You never came to the parties out here so you don't know your way around, but I did. There's a cellar entrance we all used, and

I know the interior layout of the cabin. I can get in without Pope knowing."

"Then what? You walk up to Pope and say, 'Pretty please let them go'."

Ryan ignored the sarcasm and slipped the gun from his waistband.

"You're crazy…you've only shot at a target. You don't know how to use that against someone."

"It's their only chance. You know as well as I do that Pope will kill them once he doesn't need them anymore. They've got a better chance with me."

"I don't know." Russ ran a hand around the back of his neck. "Pope might see you get out of the car."

"Not from this distance if we turn off the dome light. He doesn't know I'm with you so when you drive off he'll be fine." Ryan grabbed his brother's arm. "C'mon, Russ. I can do this. Thanks to Wally I know how to use a gun. And I have a vested interest in succeeding."

Russ stared ahead. "You won't take any chances? Put them in more danger?"

"Scout's honor."

"Don't make me regret doing this." He reached up and flipped off the dome light. "Now, get outta here."

Ryan slipped silently from the car and duckwalked into the cover of the woods bordering the drive. Waiting for Russ to turn around and head out, he concentrated on catching his breath.

What would he find inside? The sight of Cara

lying in her own blood invaded his mind. Terror pierced his heart.

Mia and other's lives depended on him. What if he failed again? He couldn't do this. Not alone anyway.

His words to Mia, trust in the Lord with all your heart and lean not on your own understanding, reverberated through his brain. What kind of a Christian was he if he told Mia to live these words, but didn't follow them himself?

As Russ's car retreated up the drive, Ryan lifted his head.

Father, I don't know why this is happening. I'm terrified for Mia and the others. I ask You to keep them safe. Help me to trust that you will keep them alive.

Waiting for miraculous intervention, Ryan eased out of his space and headed for whatever faced him in the cabin.

Mia slid down the wall next to Jessie as directed by Pope. He'd lined the four of them up like sitting ducks and that's just what she felt like. He stood at the window, his body odor from half-moons of perspiration under his arms fouling the air. He lifted blind slats then looked back at them, his eyes wild and rimmed in red.

Mia had to figure out how to get these kids out of here safely. But how? She was in over her head. Only a miracle could save them. A miracle? If Ryan were here, he'd pray. Maybe it was time she tried it, too. What could it hurt if she did?

Okay, God. We haven't talked in a long time. Things have been going kind of badly lately and I was wondering if You might help me out here. I know I don't deserve anything with how I've acted toward You, but Jessie, Eddie and Nikki need You. Send us a miracle. Show us a safe way out of here.

A loud peal of laughter snapped her eyes open. Pope stared at her, his mouth cracked in a sneer above a nonexistent chin covered with grayed whiskers. His glazed eyes said that he enjoyed inflicting terror on the innocent. She heard a car moving in the distance but her hope shriveled away as the sound of the engine receded.

He whipped his face toward the window. "That's better. The cops have turned tail and run." He cackled as he crossed the room and sat facing them in an easy chair. "Thanks for leading me here, Mia. Looks like things might work out just fine. I knew if I watched you, you'd bring me straight to my little Jessie."

His fond tone when he said Jessie's name crept along Mia's nerves and filled her with rage. The desire to lunge for his throat was nearly overwhelming. But she had to keep calm and try to manipulate him as he thought he was doing to her. Maybe if she got him talking about what he'd done, he'd get cocky and relax, giving her an opening.

"So why are you doing this?" she asked.

He arched an eyebrow that wrinkled his shaved scalp. "Thought a smart girl like you would have it all figured out by now."

"You're too good, I guess." She lightened her tone to keep him talking. "I owe you big time for that smash on my head when you plowed into me with the camera."

He smirked. "You thought you were so smart. Didn't count on me outwittin' you, did ya? All I had to do was close my eyes like you were doin'."

Anger flared inside her at his confidence. She wanted to leap across the room and claw at his smug smile.

Count to ten and blow off his snide comments, then refocus.

"Why didn't you just take off when you had a chance?"

His narrowed eyes turned mean. "That's for me to know and you to find out. Besides, we'll have lots of time for talkin' since you're gonna drive me out of here."

He thought this would scare her, but she'd willingly go with him to protect Jessie and maybe get a chance to free her.

"So tell me," she said, "how'd you find out about Jessie in the first place?"

He grinned wide, revealing a missing tooth on the right side. "Not that you're gonna make it out of here, but if you did, I'd suggest upping the security on your wireless network. Your e-mail to the good police chief proved to be very enjoyable."

Anguish shot into her. If she hadn't e-mailed Russ, Pope would never have known about Jessie. Still, there was nothing she could do about it now. She just had to keep trying things until God provided that miracle.

She tried not to let him see how upset she was over his news. "You didn't say exactly what's gonna happen now?"

He scrubbed his hand over tired eyes. "Why don't you just shut up for a while. I've got some thinkin' to do."

Mia complied. If there was any good news in all of this, it was that Pope didn't appear crazy. Mean, ornery, and a murderer, but not crazy. And that she could work with. Someone who'd gone over the edge was another story.

She tried to get Jessie's attention to give her a thumbs-up, but her head was hanging as she sobbed quietly. This man would pay for what he'd done to her. Eddie had his arm slung around Nikki, who trembled. They sat like this for what seemed like an eternity before Mia's phone rang. She looked at the caller ID.

"It's the police chief," she said.

Pope crossed the room and looked out the window. "Answer it."

"Russ."

"Is Pope listening?" Russ's voice was low, yet urgent.

"No."

"Ryan entered the house through the cellar. He should be nearby. He has a gun. Stay as far away from Pope as possible. Now tell him we've done as he asked and the road is clear."

"Okay, let me tell him." Mia looked at Pope. "The police have left. We can go now."

"Tell him I have my gun in the kid's neck. Anyone takes a shot at me, she gets it. And tell him you're driving." Pope's face took on a hard determination driving terror into Mia's heart.

Her voice trembling, she relayed the message to Russ, though he'd likely heard it over the cell.

"Okay, people," Pope shouted while gazing out the window. "On your feet."

With Pope distracted, Mia quickly signaled with her hand for the others to stay put, and she jumped up. "How about leaving them here and just taking me?"

Pope spun around. "Nah. The brat is my insurance policy. Nobody likes it when a kid gets killed."

Mia frantically scanned the room for a way to stop this madness. She spotted Ryan's reflection in a mirror. He had his gun trained on Pope, but he couldn't risk firing while Pope aimed his gun at Jessie. It was up to Mia to disarm him.

"I said for you to get up." Pope jerked the gun at Jessie ending with it aimed above her head.

Mia seized the moment. She launched into Pope, hitting his stomach with her shoulder.

He tumbled backward, pulling her down on top of him.

The gun fired.

Debris from the bullet piercing the ceiling fell on Mia. She flung her arm out, knocking the gun out of Pope's hand. The weapon slid across the wooden floor. She broke free, and lunged for it. Her fingers touched the handle.

Pope clamped a hand on her leg and pulled.

She stabbed a toe into the wood and held her ground. She reached. Slapped her hand at the gun, sending it skittering across the floor into the corner.

Pope growled and pulled hard, flipping her over. He rose up, glaring at her with fiery eyes. Veins in his neck surged to the surface, flushing his face to a raging red.

Hoping to poke him in the eye, she shot out a hand.

"Not so fast," Pope leaned on an elbow and clamped his other hand on her arm.

"Get off, Pope," Ryan bellowed. "Or so help me, I'll empty this gun on you."

Pope's eyes narrowed. He rolled to the side and studied Ryan as if surprised.

Breathing deep, Mia peered at Ryan. His eyes

burned with the same revulsion that coursed through her. She used her eyes to urge him to pull the trigger. He ran a hand over his face and his eyes cleared.

No! He was backing down. A man who treated Jessie the way Pope did, didn't deserve mercy.

Mia scrambled away like a toddler learning to walk. She spotted Pope's gun in the corner and rushed to get it. Hands shaking she stood over him and held out the gun. Her finger ached to pull the trigger.

"Mia, stop," Ryan said, placing his hand on the barrel of the gun. "He's evil, but it's not our place to judge him. God will see to that."

"God? God? Where was He when this creep took Jessie?" Mia cut her gaze at Jessie.

Nikki clutched the trembling child to her chest and covered Jessie's ears with her hand, blocking out Mia's ranting. Nikki had done the right thing. Put Jessie first. A teenager knew better than Mia did.

Mia's anger ebbed. She'd asked God to come. To send her a miracle, and He did. Right beside her in the flesh. The miracle she'd asked for. Not just any miracle, but Ryan. The man who could help her let go of all the anger and hurt from past betrayals. The man who could walk beside her and lead her in a life filled with God.

She handed the gun to Ryan and then went to Jessie. When Mia opened her arms, Nikki released Jessie and Mia clutched her.

"Ouch," Jessie said.

"Sorry," Mia said. "I'm just so glad you're all right."

"You don't have to squish me so hard." Jessie giggled and Mia knew this resilient child would be okay and so would she, if she trusted God and let Ryan into her life.

Ryan stood back watching Mia and Jessie while his pulse settled back to normal. God had come through for all of them. The pain of losing Cara would forever be etched in his heart, but he'd learned to put aside his fear and once again let God control his life.

He crossed the room to tell Mia about the answer to his prayer. To tell her he could lay down his fear of losing a woman and enter a relationship as a whole man again. Their eyes met and she launched herself into his arms.

"I prayed for a miracle," she whispered through fresh tears. "And God sent you to me. He really does love me."

She'd made her peace with God. Ryan's heart radiated with happiness.

Thank You Lord, for showing Mia Your love.

Ryan loosened his hold and searched her face. A radiant glow beamed from her eyes. A glow of contentment that had always been missing and that he was certain came from releasing control of her life to God and trusting Him fully. Maybe this meant she could also let go of her past, of how he'd hurt her, and now they had a chance for a future together.

She was the woman he wanted to go through life with. She'd always held that spot in his heart, but when she'd left, he buried the feelings deep. Pope's threat brought his love for Mia to the surface. Now he could hardly contain it.

He smiled, trying to keep it lighthearted so he didn't scare her, but keeping the love overflowing from his heart from spilling out was like stopping Niagara Falls.

He could at least keep the topic light. "So you think I'm a miracle, huh?"

"I do. If it wasn't for you I wouldn't have even thought to pray." She reached up and trailed a finger down the side of his cheek.

He willed his mind off her gentle touch. "I have a confession to make. I haven't been as trusting as I should have been."

With an encouraging smile, she urged him to go on while she softly traced his jaw, driving him mad.

He captured her hand and held it next to his heart. "The past few days spent with you made me realize how much you mean to me. But I didn't say anything because I was afraid to admit it and then lose you like I lost Cara." He paused. "Tonight has changed all of that."

She wove her fingers with his and rested her head against his chest.

Why wasn't she saying anything? Had he jumped the gun and scared her by his admission? Or worse yet, misread the signs that she might be feeling the same way?

He had to find out. "This feels so right, Mia. Like we've never been apart. We're good together."

She peered up at him, her eyes turning impish. "You think so? Even when I try to take over and do things my way?"

"Even then." He tweaked her nose. "Though as you learn to trust God more that'll probably change."

She jabbed him with a playful punch. "Trying to change me, are you?"

"Me?" He chuckled. "Seriously, Mia. You're the perfect woman for me. Always have been. Always will be." He released her hand and clamped his arms round her.

"*This* is perfect." A contented sigh slipped from her lips as she snuggled closer.

Perfect?

Almost. She hadn't actually admitted how she felt about him.

So what? Her body language told him everything he needed to know for now. He had plenty of time to convince her they belonged together. She wasn't going anywhere for the next year. He was a very persuasive man when he set his mind to it, and his mind was set on making her his wife.

TWENTY TWO

A few days later, Mia stood next to Ryan for the worship service's closing song. Today's service was so different from the ones she attended growing up. When her mom was alive, church held a place of significance in their lives. When she died, Mia's dad went through the motions of raising them in the church, but she saw the emptiness of his plan and rebelled.

As the song ended, she experienced more hope for the future than she'd had since her mom died. Incorporating her newfound faith in her everyday life would give her this peace on a regular basis.

Ryan turned to her, a timid light to his eyes. "So how was it?"

She smiled with joy. "Great, but not anything like I expected. Who knew church had changed so much since I was a kid?"

"Glad to hear you liked it." Ryan squeezed her hand.

Mia spotted Verna exiting the worship center. Mia

had asked Verna to stay on as Pinetree's manager but Verna hadn't yet responded.

She hesitantly approached Mia. "You sure you want me working at Pinetree after thinking I did all those things?"

Mia felt a blush creep over her face. "I'm sorry about that, Verna. But you were so testy, and seemed like you were trying to hide something, what was I supposed to think?"

Verna rolled her eyes. "Can't a body be worried about keeping her job? I figured you were gonna take over and send an old lady like me packing."

"Why would I do that? I wouldn't know how to run the place without you."

Verna sniffed and as a tight smile slipped out she pulled back her shoulders. "That's fine, then. I'll see you first thing in the morning."

Another wave of contentment washed over Mia.

"C'mon," Ryan said as he clasped her hand. "There's something I want you to see."

He led her to a room off the kitchen. She opened the door and a loud chorus of voices shouted, "Surprise."

Mia took a step back.

"Relax," Ryan whispered near her ear as he held her in place. "I know you don't like public demonstrations, but this is different. These people all love you and want to let you know how proud they are of what you did to save Jessie. They're our friends."

Memories of being publically grilled for her poor decisions in high school rushed to the surface. The urge to flee as she had in the past clung to her like a fabric sheet on clothes.

Ryan squeezed her shoulder. "Think of this as a start to building a life here."

She looked into his eyes and let the emanating warmth seep in. She pushed back her fear and put on a smile.

"'Bout time you got in here." Gladys rushed forward and ushered Mia into a chair at the end of the table. Gladys lifted a glass of soda to the group. "To Mia. Thank you for returning our community to the calm place we know and love. And of course, for taking care of our little Jessie."

Glasses raised around the table to calls of, "To Mia."

"Now, let's eat." Gladys clapped her hands and dishes were passed and plates heaped.

Mia wiped moist palms on her knees and took the time to look around. The table was decorated with a festive tablecloth, balloons and flowers. Of course, in Gladys's flamboyant style, everything was loud and boisterous, colors clashing. Jessie, in a pink party dress, sat at the far end of the table with Reid and Russ flanking her. Sydney, Nikki and Eddie took up the seats on one side.

Mia connected gazes with Eddie. He gave her a

shy smile and a thumbs-up. She smiled back and warmth from the joy of helping to change a life erased the last of her unease.

Ryan was right. These were her friends now. Well, maybe Eddie wasn't a friend, but they'd formed a special bond. He was far from a docile teen, but in the last few days he'd opened up and decided it would be a good idea to work on his problems.

Mia leaned closer to Ryan and tipped her head at Eddie. "We did good with that one."

"We did, didn't we?" He winked at her. "And this is just the beginning. There'll be a lot more success stories in the year to come." His lips melted into an intimate smile. "And longer if I have my way."

Her heart rate kicked up. She loved this man. She hadn't admitted that to him, but she would soon find the courage to tell him he was the perfect man for her. He'd proven she could trust him. Even when she sent him packing, he thought of her first and did what he believed to be the best thing for her.

Not only that, but his compassion and skills as a counselor translated into his relationships. He didn't let her get away with hiding from things she feared. And his smile, the one causing her stomach to flip-flop right now, was oh, so sweet. She tuned everyone else out and returned a smile that she hoped conveyed her heart's desire.

"Mia," Gladys tugged on her arm then bent down to whisper, "I think it's time you took this man home and told him how you feel."

Instead of irritating Mia, Gladys had read her mind. Eyes locked on a flushed Ryan, Mia hastily made their excuses and they ran to his truck together. Not wanting to talk and break the mood, Mia clutched his hand for the ride.

As they approached the lodge, she pointed out the front window of the truck. "Someone's here."

Ryan pulled the truck to a stop and turned to face her. His adoring eyes locked with hers. "I didn't want to tell you about this earlier because I thought it would keep you from enjoying the party."

"That sounds ominous."

He laughed. "Not at all. When I heard your dad and David turned down the invitation to come to the party, I went to see them."

"But you had—"

He held up his hand. "Wait, before you say anything else. You know I want you to be happy living here. I don't think you could ever really settle down here unless you reconciled with your family. So I talked to them. They didn't come to the party because they wanted to meet with you in private."

She peered out the window and contemplated an escape. What if she went in and they turned away from her again? What if nothing had changed? For the second time this afternoon, she wanted to run. But what good would that do?

At the very least, she should throttle Ryan for interfering and trying to control her future. She swiveled on the patched seat and looked into his eyes. All she saw was concern and maybe if she were lucky, love. He wasn't trying to control her like her dad had in the past, he was trying to make her happy.

Her throat thick with trepidation, she swallowed hard. "Will you go in with me?"

"You know I will." He escorted her to the door and pushed it open.

She stepped across the threshold and stopped. A large portrait of her mother that used to hang above their fireplace at home was perched on the long mantel. As if in a dream, Mia entered the family room and her gaze flew around the space taking in special items of her mother's scattered about.

"We thought you'd like to have these things from the storage unit," David said, coming forward.

Tears rose in her eyes as she nodded. "Thank you."

"Mia." Her father crossed the room and stood in front of her. His eyes were moist and contrite. "I was so wrong to try to erase the memory of your mother. The pain of her loss was," his voice caught, "*is* still almost too much to bear. I pushed you away when I should have reached out. Can you forgive me and give me another chance?"

Now that the moment she'd waited years for had come, she didn't know how to react other than to stare into the warm, loving eyes of a father whose gaze had only registered coldness for ten years. Ten long years of pain.

She couldn't fall into his arms as if nothing happened, but thanks to her renewed faith, she could forgive him and give him another chance. "I'd like it if we got to know each other."

His body sagged with relief, and he held out his hand. "How about we start by looking at your mom's things together?"

Mia shared a peaceful look with Ryan then accepted her father's hand. David joined them at the counter where her mother's jewelry box sat open and filled with treasures Mia had played with as a child. They spent the afternoon sharing good memories and talking about plans for a future.

With a promise to get together again, her father and David left.

She plopped on the sofa and sighed. "This has been the best day."

"I agree." Ryan sat next to her and circled his arm around her shoulders.

She slid closer settling into the curve and laying her head on his chest. "Even better," she whispered into his neck.

He drew her closer. She reveled in the warmth of their connection and the beating of his heart, strong and solid beneath her head. He loved her. At least she thought he did.

After he rescued them from Pope, Ryan had intimated that he loved her and wanted to spend the rest of his life with her, but he hadn't said another word since then. He hadn't officially declared his love, asking her to stay in Logan Lake, or even tried to hold her or kiss her. Was she wrong about him?

Looking up at him, she relived the last few days. His strong arms as he carried her from the fire, the concern in his voice each time he tried to warn her to be careful and his joyful face when she revealed her renewed faith. And now, his captivating blue eyes telegraphing a message she hoped was love.

But maybe he didn't love her. Maybe he regretted what he'd said at the cabin. Her counseling experience told her that when people survived an intense incident like the one they'd gone through, they often said things that they didn't mean in the heat of the moment.

Maybe Ryan had simply felt relief that he could save her life, and in that moment, he'd confused his feelings with love. Or maybe he was waiting for her to tell him how she felt.

Could she do that? Could she let down all the walls she'd erected for ten years and tell him she loved him? Because she did. More than she ever could have imagined she'd love a man.

She sighed.

"What?" he asked. "What's wrong?"

Here was her opening.

His tender gaze fixed on her face and sent warmth radiating to her very soul. She should be able to say the three little words, but when she opened her mouth to speak, she froze.

"You look terrified of something," Ryan said.

"I am."

His eyebrows drew together, and he leaned back. "Is it about your father?"

She shook her head.

His compelling blue eyes turned questioning as he loosened his hold on her. "About us? Together, like this?"

"Yes," she whispered and waited for him to acknowledge his mistake in admitting he cared for her.

"This isn't something to be afraid of. It's something to celebrate." He caressed her cheek with a calloused hand. "After I sent you away, I didn't think I'd find you again. Ten years since we saw each other and it feels like we've never been apart."

Ten years. Such a long time to spend searching for what she'd already had.

"We wasted so much time," she said.

"Don't think that way. God used that time to mold us into the people we are today. We both needed to grow up to recognize what we have together is special." He cupped her face and held her in a mesmerizing trance. "I love you, Mia. More than I can say."

She felt tears form, and her heart explode with joy, but before she could respond, he withdrew his hands and crossed the room.

What?

He lifted his jacket from the back of a chair.

"Wait!" She jumped to her feet and raced toward him. "Don't go, Ryan. I love you, too. Please don't leave."

"I'm not leaving." He dug into the pocket of his jacket. "I've been trying to be patient for the past few days and not scare you off, but I can't wait any longer." From his pocket, he pulled out a blue velvet box and knelt in front of her. "I love you Mia, and I don't want you to leave Logan Lake again. Will you stay and be my wife?"

"Is this for real?" Her face burned with excitement, and she waved her hand to cool her skin.

Searching her eyes, he opened the box and held it out. "You didn't answer."

Overwhelming emotions wouldn't allow her to speak so she dropped to the floor next to him and drew his head close, letting her kiss answer his question. His lips lingered and the kiss nearly stopped her heart but she'd never felt more alive.

He pulled back and held out the ring. "That felt like yes, but I need to hear the word."

"Yes. Yes. Yes." She stopped at three, but the way his eyes met hers in a loving caress, she wanted to shout yes a thousand times.

As he slid the ring on her finger, the past ten years of heartache slipped from her mind. Never had she felt more at home, more at peace. She'd risked everything in coming back to Pinetree to inherit the place. But instead of a place, she'd inherited a family who would see her through good times and bad. Ryan had proven he'd always be there for her, and no matter what the future brought they would face it together.

* * * * *

Dear Reader,

Trusting in God. Wow, that's so easy to say, yet so hard to do when faced with life-altering challenges like Mia and Ryan experienced. I've been there more times than I care to count. When worry and the urge to take control overpower my trust in God.

And that's why I chose to write this book. To share through Mia and Ryan that no matter the problem, when we trust in the Lord and don't try to take things into our own hands, He has a far richer and more rewarding life planned for us than we could ever dream on our own.

I pray that the book has encouraged you to trust in the Lord no matter the difficulty you face. I love to hear from readers and you can reach me through my Web site, www.susansleeman.com, or in care of Steeple Hill Books at 233 Broadway, Suite 1001, New York, NY 10279.

Susan Sleeman

QUESTIONS FOR DISCUSSION

1. Mia didn't want to return to Logan Lake and face people who had hurt her. Do you have people in your past that you don't want to see? Should you and how can you overcome this fear?

2. Mia, Ryan and Mia's father take years to recover from the loss of a loved one. Not all loss is this profound, but we experience losses every day. Have you ever experienced such a terrible loss and how did you cope with it?

3. Mia's rejection by her father caused her to struggle with trust. This happened at a vulnerable age when she was forming many of her coping skills in life. She transferred the feeling of betrayal from her father to God and was unable to trust Him. How has your relationship with your father impacted how you see your heavenly Father?

4. Each time Mia sees her father she is tempted to run away and hide from the pain. Have you ever been tempted to run from a painful issue? How have you overcome the temptation to flee? How did you learn to stand firm and face your issue?

5. Ryan lost the woman he was to marry, leaving him fearful. Have you ever had something terrible happen that left you fearful that it would

happen again? If so, how did you handle it? Were you proud of the way you handled it? If not, how would God want you to handle it?

6. Ryan let Mia go in high school because he loved her. Have you ever had to make a decision that hurt someone you loved, but it was in their best interest? How did this make you feel? Did you ever get the chance to let the person know why you did it?

7. Ryan and Mia both tried to prevent bad things from happening by taking control of their lives. Have you ever taken control of your life? Is this what God wants you to do?

8. Trust, once broken, is so hard to reclaim. Have you ever been in a relationship where someone has done something to lose your trust? Did they ever regain it and if so, how? If you are experiencing this problem right now, how can your faith help you through it?

9. When Mia sees Ryan for the first time, every thought about what she was going to say to him and how she would behave around him fled from her mind. Have you ever pictured how an interaction with someone will go and then find it to play out differently than you pictured? How did you handle the situation?

10. Mia and Ryan both sought counseling careers where they could help people. Why do you think both of them became counselors when they had so many unresolved issues to deal with in their own lives? Though you may not be a counselor, can you use situations you've worked through in your life to help others?

11. In the time that Mia and Ryan were apart, Ryan developed his relationship with God when Mia walked away. If Mia hadn't learned to trust God again, do you think the two of them could have gotten back together? Have you ever had a time in your life where your faith has grown beyond those around you? Was this difficult and how did you handle it?

12. *High-Stakes Inheritance* is based on *Proverbs* 3:5: Trust in the Lord with all your heart and lean not on your own understanding. If Mia and Ryan had employed this verse earlier in their lives, how would their lives have been different? Do you struggle with trusting God like this? What steps can you take to trust Him more?

LARGER-PRINT BOOKS!

**GET 2 FREE
LARGER-PRINT NOVELS
PLUS 2 FREE
MYSTERY GIFTS**

Love Inspired®
SUSPENSE
RIVETING INSPIRATIONAL ROMANCE

Larger-print novels are now available...

HEARTWARMING INSPIRATIONAL ROMANCE

Contemporary,
inspirational romances
with Christian characters
facing the challenges
of life and love
in today's world.

**NOW AVAILABLE IN REGULAR
AND LARGER-PRINT FORMATS.**

Steeple
Hill®

Love Inspired.
HISTORICAL
INSPIRATIONAL HISTORICAL ROMANCE

Engaging stories of romance,
adventure and faith,
these novels are set in
various historical periods
from biblical times
to World War II.

NOW AVAILABLE!

Steeple
Hill®